Jean Paul

The Doctrine of Education

Jean Paul

The Doctrine of Education

ISBN/EAN: 9783742811967

Manufactured in Europe, USA, Canada, Australia, Japa

Cover: Foto ©Andreas Hilbeck / pixelio.de

Manufactured and distributed by brebook publishing software
(www.brebook.com)

Jean Paul

The Doctrine of Education

JEAN PAUL FRIEDRICH RICHTER'S
LEVANA

OR,

THE DOCTRINE OF EDUCATION

FOR ENGLISH READERS.

BY

SUSAN WOOD, B.Sc.

(Formerly Head-Mistress of the Bath High School for Girls.)

" L'homme n'est ni ange ni bête ; et le malheur veut que qui veut faire l'ange fait la bête."—*Pascal.*

LONDON :

SWAN SONNENSCHEIN, LOWREY & CO.,

PATERNOSTER SQUARE.

1887.

Butler & Tanner,
The Selwood Printing Works,
Frome, and London.

To the

PARENTS AND TEACHERS OF OUR CHILDREN

THIS

STRING OF PEARLS FROM A FOREIGN LAND

IS AFFECTIONATELY DEDICATED

BY

ONE OF THEIR FRIENDS.

CONTENTS.

FIRST FRAGMENT.

FOURTH FRAGMENT.

ON FEMALE EDUCATION.

FIFTH FRAGMENT.

EDUCATION OF A PRINCE.

SIXTH FRAGMENT.

MORAL EDUCATION OF BOYS.

SEVENTH FRAGMENT.

Contents.

INTRODUCTION.

_____

" IT is good to repeat old thoughts in the
" newest books, because the old works in
" which they stand are not read."

With these words does Richter justify himself for presenting to the world his " Theory
of Education," and the same thought gave
birth to the present form of his work.

Even Germans find that Richter's highly
metaphorical style makes heavy demands on
their attention ; and for that reason, although
several English translations exist, it is not
strange to find the " Levana" somewhat
neglected by our own Educationists, although
prescribed to be read for the " Teacher's
" Diploma " in 1886 by the University of
London.

It has been the present translator's object
to gather out some of the pregnant sayings
with which the book abounds, and to thread

them together in such a way as to exhibit
the current of the author's ideas, whilst
avoiding his numerous digressions. The
work lends itself readily to such treatment,
for Richter himself in the Preface impresses
upon his readers the vastness of the subject
and the necessarily fragmentary character of
any contributions to it. In fact, he calls the
subdivisions of his book " Fragments" ; and
in these fragments no one topic is treated
exhaustively, but the thoughts of the author
are expressed like Pascal's " Pensées," in
the form of aphorisms, which, being the
utterances of a true philosopher and poet,
illuminate as with a lightning-flash the in-
tricate problems of education and of life.

In the seventeenth century Pascal's dictum
was that : " L'homme n'est ni ange ni bête ;
" et le malheur veut que qui veut faire l'ange
" fait la bête." A century later Richter pro-
claimed as his belief that " Each generation
" starts afresh from Paradise."

Others were at work in the same field.
His own birth (in 1763) took place a year

after the publication of Rousseau's "Emile";
his death (1825) preceded by two years the
death of Pestalozzi, who was just beginning
his work at Yverdun at the time that Richter
was writing his "Levana," which was printed
in 1806. School-instruction in Germany was
as yet in the swaddling-bands of tradition,
for although Frederic the Great had done
somewhat to improve the inspection of schools
in Prussia, and had made them nominally in-
stitutions of the State, yet the great reforms
of Falk were still in the future, and the first
kindergarten was not opened until 1840.
Whether the thorough organization of instruction in Germany during the last fifteen
years, together with the development of
Froebel's system, would have modified
Richter's views, or any part of his treatise,
it is impossible to say. But unquestionably
his work, dealing as it does with education
in its widest sense, can never lose its value.

The subject of education was evidently
much in his mind. In several of his ro-
mances teachers are the heroes, and scattered

throughout his works are statements and aphorisms that may be claimed by pedagogic science. He came of a stock of school-masters. His grandfather was Rector (Head Master) of a public school, and his father, during a few years, assistant in one. He, himself, twice in his early manhood, under-took work as a tutor. The failure of his efforts in the first attempt and the success of the second period spent in teaching (1790–94), both left their mark on himself; and "Levana" owes its conception to those years, though it was not written until after he had become a father, and, as he himself tells us, " gained in maturity through his own chil-" dren."

Of his work as an author in general, it would be out of place to speak, and the chief events of his life are well known; a short account of his experiences as a teacher may, however, be interesting in this connection. At the time when he was vainly striving to find a publisher for his early books, and struggling with the direst poverty under his widowed mother's roof, he accepted the post of private tutor to a younger brother of his friend, Adam von Oerthel. He found, however, his pupil dull and unreceptive, both of intellectual and moral culture, and the father of the boy purse-proud and uncongenial. He left this post on the death of his friend, at the end of two years. The second experience was of a very different kind. After refusing several offers of similar work, Richter at last consented to take charge of the children of a friend at Schwachenbach, whom he was to educate with those of some other families in that town. For four or five years he worked with these seven pupils, whose ages varied from six to fifteen.

His biographer Spazier says of him: "The "individuality, depth, and greatness of a true "poet-nature has never been exemplified so "plainly as by Jean Paul's direction and "organization of this little school, and by "its reaction on his own being. What to an "ordinary man, even the most talented, is a "fettering, or even a deadening occupation,—

" the daily instruction of little children in
" the very first elements of knowledge,—this
" occupation opened to him all the sources
" of elevated and great thoughts, hastened
" and completed the development of his survey
" of the universe, fanned his sensitive and
" active fancy into clear flames, and supplied
" it at the same time with its first artistic
" material.

" He could not help considering and treat-
" ing his pupils as living forms of a poetic
" world. He felt obliged to pour forth to
" them all that he had gathered as the result
" of his meditations, and the suggestions of
" the inspired moments of his poet-soul, con-
" cerning man, the world, his own life and
" heart,—to implant all this in the children's
" souls, receptive as wax of every impression.
" The gain to himself was incalculable, and
" so was the ever-increasing enjoyment with
" which he performed his work in this ap-
" parently heterodox way. If anything shows
" the unusual greatness of his poetic talents,
" it is that he was able to use such a relation-

" ship in such a manner that a children's
" schoolroom became for him not merely a
" Socratic Academy, but also a School of
" Poetry and Art. Hence we find, through-
" out Jean Paul's methods of education and
" instruction, the poet reproducing himself
" in all his pupils, however different their age
" and talents. As two of them happily ex-
" pressed it, he was the planet Saturn, and
" they were the seven satellites."

His aim was to give his pupils the help
which his father and schoolmasters seem to
have failed to give to him, and which he
tells us in his autobiography he had so
earnestly longed for. He desired to supply
them with sufficient variety of mental food,
together with subjects of knowledge ade-
quately simple. He also led them to make
use of all they learnt, to rearrange their
materials as he himself had done. In one
word, his whole method consisted in directing
the children along the path of discovery and
creation for themselves. In his " Levana " he
calls this method " the awakening of the

" conceptive power, a spiritual impulse, which,
" more lofty than the physical, by degrees
" creates new ideas out of the old, under the
" direction of the will."

During five hours daily he instructed his
pupils in German, Latin, French, English,
and in the so-called practical sciences. The
repetition lessons gave him an opportunity
of bringing together various facts and ideas
arising out of these manifold subjects of
instruction, and thus of connecting one with
another; and he encouraged his pupils at
such times to seek express witty analogies,
derived from their various studies. They
were not allowed to interrupt the lesson, but
a set time was appointed in which the
scholars expressed their "happy thoughts."
Jean Paul kept a special book for the sayings
of his pupils, calling it the " Bon-mot-antho-
" logie," specimens of which appear in the
" Levana."

The notion of encouraging the production
of original ideas was not altogether new,
having been already suggested by Rousseau

and Pestalozzi. But new and peculiar to himself was the method above described for realizing his object. The great importance attached by him to wit and to its training, is to be explained by the history of his own development, in the course of which he was for a long time obliged to obtain mental stimulus from this source.

Jean Paul laid special stress on the written exercises of the pupils. He considered the writing down of mental productions to be the most suitable means for developing the "con- " ceptive power," because, as he says, " writing " elevates the signs of things into things " themselves, and throws more light upon " ideas than speaking does." Hence he gave his scholars as many opportunities, and as much encouragement as possible, for writing. In this he merely followed the plan of his own self-culture, in which the filling of MS. books with excerpts from books read had played a prominent part. In his autobio- graphy he gives details of the large amount of voluntary work done by some of his little pupils, consisting of many sheets of translations and essays. Concerning these exercises Wirth remarks that " it is not strange that " so original a teacher should have carried " his pupils with him by his thoughts, his " language, the attraction of his sympathy; " and that he should have roused their ambi- " tion and spurred them on to the greatest " industry and zeal. It is to be regretted " that we have no more exact account of the " kind and contents of the essays mentioned. " Whether, however, they were original or " mere reproductions of the instruction re- " ceived, the amount seems excessive and " unnatural."

No doubt, if Richter had made teaching his profession, he would have modified his plans as time went on. Even in the case of a great genius, the work of a 'prentice-hand is apt to want balance. It would be interesting to know something of the fruits of his labours, but unfortunately nothing of the after-life of his pupils has been disclosed to us except that the two eldest died in their youth.

The effect of this period on himself is less doubtful, as his biographers in passages already quoted, and in many similar ones, have shown. From his tutor experiences he gained ideas and thoughts which developed into a thousand forms in his works. If "the "noblest study of mankind is man," every poet and philosopher must take an eager interest in the early life of human beings, as well as in the influences that contribute to and aid in their development. If each new generation starts indeed " afresh from Para- "dise," what golden opportunities are in the hands of those who guide the tottering steps of the little ones! Shall we say it is enough that they should follow the hard-beaten tracks made by us and our fathers? Are we so sure that these paths lead to any new Eden? Is there not possibly a more excellent way?

The " Levana " suggests these and many like thoughts. Full of great ideas, apt illustrations, lofty principles, yet courageously free from all absolute rules,—which he explicitly deprecates in his Preface,—the book must needs inspire educators of children— be they parents or tutors—with enthusiasm, together with a solemn sense both of the importance and difficulty of their work.

Let the author himself speak, as from the unseen world :

" It would be my greatest reward if, at the " end of twenty years, some reader as many " years old should return thanks to me that " the book which he is then reading had " been read by his parents." . . .

- " May 'Levana,' the motherly goddess who " was formerly entreated to give a father's " heart to fathers, hear the prayer which the " title of the book addresses to her, and jus- " tify both it and this ! "

LEVANA;

or,

DOCTRINE OF EDUCATION.

———◆◆———

FIRST FRAGMENT.

Chapter I.

When Antipater demanded of the Spartans fifty
children as hostages, one hundred distinguished men
were offered him in their stead. Ordinary educators
are apt to reverse the sacrifice.

These words form the keynote of Chapter
I., which is concerned with the importance
of education. Our author bases it upon the
fact that children represent posterity to us,
while, at the same time, they start as it were
afresh from Paradise. The present genera-

tion therefore has the making of posterity in its hands.

In the world of children the whole afterworld lies before us, into which we, like Moses into the Promised Land, may gaze, but not enter; and again, it renews for us the childhood of the world which we have left far behind.

By education, we sow upon a pure soft soil plants bearing either poisoned fruits or honey-glands; and as the gods descended to primitive men, so do we—giants physically and spiritually in our children's eyes—descend to these little ones, and make them great or small. . . . How do you know whether the little boy who is plucking flowers at your side may not one day from his island of Corsica come forth as a war-god into a stormy world, in order to play with the storms; to destroy, or to purify and renew? Would it be indifferent to you whether you were his Fénélon or his Cornelia or his Dubois? For although you cannot destroy or direct the power of genius,—the deeper the sea, the steeper the coast,—yet, in the consecrating all-important decade of life,—the first,—at the dawn of all emotions, you may surround and restrain the couching lion's strength with all the tender habits of a gentle heart, with all the bonds of love. Whether an angel or a devil educate that great genius is of far more importance than whether a learned Doctor or a Charles the Simple teach him.

Not that our author would have us suppose that the education of geniuses is alone of importance.

The mass of average men who are acted upon are as important as the leading spirits who act on them. . . . By means of the child, that is, of the short arm of the lever of Humanity, you set in motion a long one whose wide arc your eye can hardly trace in the height and depth of Time.

Chapter II.

The author puts himself in the place of an imaginary opponent, and discusses the question whether the education of home and school can after all effect much.

It may be argued that children closely resemble their parents, as all history teaches us. The ancients did little for children, their schools were for growing youths. The man was lost in the State. The State was therefore the chief educator. Again, in all times the most powerful influence comes from the spirit of the nation and of the age.

The living time, which with so many thousand men,

by means of events and opinions, incessantly for twenty or thirty years tosses the human being to and fro as with a sea of waves, must soon wash away or cover over the deposit of the few short school-years, in which spoke only one man, and only words.

The century is the spiritual climate of man, the school-years are the hot-house and forcing-pit out of which he is taken to be planted out for ever. . . . What can isolated words do against living, present action ? The present has new words for new deeds; the teacher had only dead language for his corpse-like examples. . . . The present age never ceases in its action for a moment, and it seizes upon us with joy and sorrow, with towns and books, with friends and enemies; in short, with thousand-handed life.

CHAPTER III.

Having shown how little what is usually called education can do by comparison with the experience of life, we may return to establish its importance by counter-consider-ations.

The invention of printing has transformed the world; this we must bear in mind when we study the modes of life among the ancients. Again, we must never forget that the years of childhood are *the* impressionable years of both heart and brain.

Life, especially moral life, has a flight, then a leap, then a step, then a halt. . . . A warm drop has power to cause the hard seed of childhood to swell and grow, whilst a whole shower of rain does little to nourish an outspread leafy tree. . . . Two forces are at work: first, the trust of childhood, this imbibing power without which no education, no language, would be possible, but the child would be like a young bird taken too late from the leafy nest, which will starve, because it will not open its beak to the fostering hand. The second power is the child's excitability, which, as in its body, so in its mind, exists in the highest degree in the morning of life, and declines with age, until at last nothing in the empty world excites the worn-out man except his future state.

Richter then shows that the mass of the nation has little direct influence on the child, but the few individuals he comes in contact with make his world. Again, the uniformity of the masses,—the inevitable likeness of children to parents which has been often insisted on,—is deceptive. The smoothness of the globe is due to a distant view; when near we see the irregularities.

SECOND FRAGMENT.

Chapter I.

THIS sets forth the need of an ideal of education.

The goal must be known before the path can be recognised. All means and arts of education will be determined by the Ideal or archetype we set before us.

The inconsistency of parents in this respect is dwelt upon, especially as regards the moral precepts they instil into their children.

If these were put into words and laid down as a time-table of studies, they would read somewhat in this fashion. First hour : Pure morality. Second : Mixed, or applicable to one's own advantage. Third : " Do you see that your father acts thus ? " Fourth : " You are little, and this is suitable only for adults." Fifth : The chief thing is that you should get on in the world. Sixth : " Not the temporal, but the eternal determines the worth of a man," and so on. .   .

Again, many parents educate their children only for themselves, to be fine machines, soul-alarums, which are not set going so long as quiet is needed. The child is each moment to be merely that on which the educator can sleep most softly, or drum most loudly; and which, by bringing forth fruits where no seed has been sown, may spare him every moment the trouble of educating, since he has something else to do and enjoy. Hence these sluggards are frequently angry because the child is not wiser, gentler, and more consistent than themselves. Even the most zealous lovers of children are often like inflammable gas, which gives light itself but extinguishes every other.

Scarcely better than these " machinemakers " are those who would educate men to take their part in the huge machine of the State, each doing one kind of work and no other.

But the man comes before the citizen.

Education then needs an ideal. But our ideals are (as is shown) limited by our knowledge. Thus, a modern Greek might consider that his country had reached the height of civilization until he reads the story of Marathon.

The Ideal man that any nation or majority of any people has embodied and shown forth in its glory, must dwell and breathe in each individual, else he would not recognise in it a kindred being. And so indeed it is. Each of us has in himself his Ideal Man, which he secretly strives either to set free or to enchain from his youth upwards. Each one beholds this holy soul-spirit most clearly in the blossoming time of all powers, in the season of youth. For so far as we believe in any contemporaneous growth and interaction of body and soul, we must allow that the blooming time of both is the same. . . . The universal complaint : what might I not have become ! confesses the present or past existence of an oldest Adam of Paradise, along with and before the old Adam himself. But the Ideal Man comes to this earth as it were petrified—enclosed within a stone—to break this stony covering from so many limbs that the rest can free themselves, this is, or might be, education. . . . We must, however, first realize what we mean by the Ideal. Men are cast in diverse moulds. The ideal-self of Fénélon, so full of love and strength ; the ideal-self of Cato the younger, so full of strength and love, could not have been exchanged without spiritual suicide.

Consequently the problem of education is announced to be

To discover and to appreciate the individuality of the Ideal Man.

This is given as the heading of the second chapter.

CHAPTER II.

The infinite variety in human character, as in all other works of Nature, is dwelt upon. The teacher must not aim at making his pupil a reproduction of himself. He must not confound the Ideal with ideals.

As no finite thing can repeat the infinite ideality, but only mirror it back in parts, such parts must be infinitely diverse; neither the dew-drop, nor the mirror, nor the ocean gives the sun in all its fulness, but they each reflect it round and bright.

The individuality of the ideal, having been clearly apprehended as existing in the man of genius, but in every human being, has to be protected and encouraged to develope.*

---

* Cf. Carlyle: "The meaning of life here on earth might be defined as consisting in this: to unfold yourself, to work at what thing you have faculty for. It is a necessity for the human being, the first law of existence."

The author says in his Preface :—

Although the Spirit of Education, always watching over the whole, is nothing more than an endeavour to liberate, by means of a free man, the ideal human being which lies concealed in every child; and though in the application of the divine to the child's nature, it must scorn some useful things, some seasonable, individual or immediate ends; yet it must incorporate itself in the most definite applications, in order to be clearly manifested.

Intellectual tendencies are to be given free play, and weight added to special aptitudes.

The teacher has to separate from the individuality which he allows to grow, another which he must bend or guide; the one is of the head, the other is of the heart. The former must be treated as a melody, the latter as a harmony. You must not engraft a Petrarch on an Euler, for no intellectual power can become too great in its own line. But every moral faculty must be balanced by others ; let it be a law that, since every faculty is holy, none must be weakened in itself, but only the opposing one aroused, by means of which it may be added harmoniously to the whole. Thus, for instance, a too-weakly affectionate heart is not to be hardened, but the sense of honour and purity strengthened in it; the rash character not to be made timid, but only loving and wise.

The conditions under which the character of the ideal-self in each is to be developed, the author allows to be difficult to put into words ; he therefore suggests a new aspect of the end of education—

To elevate the child above the spirit of the age.

To educate, that is, not for the present— for this is done unceasingly by other influences without our aid—but for the remote future, and often in opposition to the immediate future.

This gives rise to a discussion as to the meaning of the " Spirit of the Age," which forms the subject of Chapter III.

CHAPTER III.

What is the Age ? Is it the century in which we ourselves live ? Is it the period between one great event and another ? And what kind of revolution, moral or political, will mark the epochs ? Is the "spirit of the age " the spirit of your own country or of others ? Is it not fleeting, changing, while we think of it ? And how can we, dwelling in the very midst of this same age, raise ourselves out of and above it so as

to view it as a whole? If we could view the present
in its true light, we could prognosticate the future as
our ancestors have thought to do by calling the spirit
of the age "signs of the Last Day," etc.

The author decides that his own age is
specially characterised by the union of men
with loss of individuality, and by the over-
cultivation of the passions. Men are, however, at all times ready to lament over the
degeneracy of their contemporaries. A just
view is attained if we remember that every
one regards his own age as intellectually
better and morally worse than it is, for—

In science the new (appears) always an advance, in
morals a retrogression, in contradiction to our inner
ideals and our historic idols. Yet it is true that
among nations the head has always preceded the heart
by centuries; witness the opinions concerning the
slave-trade and war. . . .

What is the cure for evil modes of life and of
thought? Sorrow is the cure of nations as of individuals, we pass through winter to the spring. That our
children may pass into that spring-time we must " arm
them with three forces, of Will, of Love, of Religion."
Our age has only passionate desires instead of will.
. . . The girl and the boy must learn that there is

something in the ocean higher than its waves—a Christ who speaks to and controls them. . . . When the stoic energy of Will is formed, the loving spirit is already made more free. Man is created for love; selfishness is a parasite that only exists on decayed plants. Let the bodily heart be the pattern of the spiritual; easily injured, sensitive, active, and warm, it is yet a tough, ever-vibrating muscle, behind a lattice-work of bones, and its delicate nerves are hard to find. . . .

There is no contest about the nature of Will and Love, but only about the ways to attain them. Concerning religion there is more dispute. Will and Love are two opposing forces of the inner man; religion the divine union of both, and the Man within the man.

Chapter IV.

When writing on religious education, Richter deplores the decay of national religion—

Religion is no longer a national, but a household goddess. . . . Posterity will dwell more and more in the street and in the market-place; it behoves us more zealously than ever to give our children a house of prayer within the heart, and folded hands, and humility before the invisible world.

Religion and morality are not the same,

though the highest degree of each becomes
the other.

Religion is the belief in God. " God is," in the
words of Sebastian Frank, " an unutterable sigh lying
in the depths of the soul. Religion is, in the beginning, the learning about God; it is rightly divine
blessedness. Without God, I am lonely throughout
eternity;* but if I have my God, I am more strengthened than by friendship and love. . . . In the
midst of impurity or the empty whirl of trifles and of
sins, in the market-place or on the battle-field, I stand
with closed breast, in which the All-mighty and All-
holy speaks to me, and rests before me like a sun,
behind which the outer world lies in darkness. I have
entered into His church, the temple of the universe,
and remain there devoutly pious though the temple
should become dark, or cold, or undermined with
graves. What I do or suffer is no sacrifice to Him, as
little as I could offer one to myself ; I love Him simply
whether I suffer or not. The flame from heaven falls
on the altar and consumes the beast, but the priest and
the flame remain. . . . A code of morals rules
only bad loveless souls, that they may become first

* Cf. Professor Clifford : " I feel the spring sun-
shine is poured from an empty heaven upon a soulless
world, and the Great Companion is dead."

better, then good. But the loving contemplation of the
Friend of the soul banishes not merely evil thoughts
that conquer, but those also which tempt. As the
eagle hovers over the highest mountains, so does true
Love over slowly-climbing Duty. . . . .

How is the child to be led into this world of religion? Not by arguments. Every step of earthly
knowledge can be climbed by learning and perseverance; but the Infinite, which supports the rungs of
the ladder, can be contemplated, not counted; we
reach it with wings, not steps. To prove the being
of God, as to doubt it, is to prove or doubt the being
of Being. . . . The Ideal is before the Real. We
have nothing for the purpose of communicating ideas
of infinity of God, but words, which can only arouse
these ideas, not create them. A whole system of religious metaphysics sleeps within the child; for man
does not properly rise to the highest, but first sinks down
and then rises up again. If Rousseau will present to us
God, and hence religion, only as the late inheritance
of a full-grown age, then he cannot expect religious
enthusiasm and love from it,—except in the case of
great souls,—any more than a Parisian father can expect
filial love from a son who appears for the first time
before him when he no longer needs a father. How
can you plant the holiest more fitly than in the holiest
time of innocence, or that which is to have influence
for ever, better than in this period of life, when nothing
is forgotten? . . .

But the teacher must have what he would give in this as in all else. . . .

Symbols of the unspeakable are better than words for young children. The sublime is the Temple-step. . . .

When what is mighty appears in nature, a storm, the starry firmament, death, then utter the word "God" before the child. A great misfortune, a great blessing, a great crime, a noble deed—these are the sites for an infant's church. . . .

Show everywhere the boundaries of the Holy Land of religion, that the child may be awed with you without knowing why. Newton, who uncovered his head when he named the Holy Name, would have been —without words—a true religious teacher of infants.

Richter deprecates the teaching of stated prayers and catechisms to children. They should go to church but rarely; the empty church is best for them, that they may see the holy place of their elders.

Reverence for foreign religions is to be taught, as forms which may enshrine the Holy of Holies to others.

Real unbelief relates to no individual propositions, or counter-propositions, but consists in blindness towards the whole. Excite in the child the all-powerful perception of the whole in opposition to the selfish, perception of the parts, and thus you raise the man above the world, the eternal above the transitory.

THIRD FRAGMENT.

CHAPTER I.

CONTAINS a digression upon the beginning of man and education.

Education begins with the first breath of the child. The dawn of life should be protected from all that is rough and violent, even from too sweet expériences.

The first three years are recognised by Richter as forming a well-marked period, for as yet speech is wanting.

The first, the three early years, like the academic Triennum, after which the gate of the soul, language, is opened, are the object of care and observation. Here, educators are the hours that open or close the gates of heaven. Here is [true] education, the unfolding, yet possible ; by means of which the long second, the curative, or counter-education, may be spared. For the child—yet in native innocence, before

18

his parents have become the serpents on the tree—
speechless, inaccessible to the poison of words—led by
customs, not by words and reasons, therefore all the
more easily moved on the narrow and small pinnacle
of sensuous experience, for the child, I say, on this
boundary-line between the man and the ape, the most
important era of his life is contained in these years in
which he for the first time colours and moulds himself
by companionship with others.

Every new educator effects less than his predecessor;
until at last, if we regard the whole of life as an educational institution, a circumnavigator of the world gains
less culture from all nations taken together than from
his nurse.

This is the age when the child is being
educated through its senses, which are in
full vigour, but require training in fine dis-
criminations. The common experiences of
life do this for taste and smell, and to a
great extent for touch, hearing, and sight.

These first three years require spiritual
" warmth " rather than " nourishment."
The care of the educator is to provide the
former, namely, an atmosphere of happiness.

Chapter II.

Cheerfulness is to be encouraged in every way.

But joyousness is not to be confounded with enjoyments. Every enjoyment, even the refined one of a work of art, gives a man a selfish aspect; and is a condition of necessity, not of virtue. On the other hand, cheerfulness, the opposite of ill-temper and gloom, is at once the soil and flower of virtue. . . . Animals can enjoy, but men alone can be cheerful. God Himself is the All-blessed. Children ought to inhabit Paradise. But pleasures make no Paradise, they only help to laugh it away. Play, that is activity, will keep children cheerful. By pleasure I understand every first agreeable sensation; a plaything gives pleasure at first by its appearance, and cheerfulness only by its use. Small pleasures often repeated are better for a young child than great ones, and a variety of pleasures should never be allowed in quick succession. Later on special festivals will illuminate many dark days. . . . Cheerfulness gives strength, as sadness takes it away. The early blossoms of joy are not corn-flowers among the seed, but young ears of corn. It is a beautiful tradition that the Virgin Mary and the poet Tasso never wept as children.

CHAPTER III.

Deals with children's games.

Unlike the games of adults, they are expressions of earnest activity, but clothed with lightest wings. Richter divides them into two classes :

(1) exertions of the receptive power, (2) of the active, formative power. One class acts like the afferent nerves, the other like the efferent. Many actions of children that are not usually spoken of as games are of the first class. Children love to move things, put keys into locks, watch the employments, listen to the conversation of their elders.

To the second class belong all those games in which the child seeks to work off his superabundant activity of mental and bodily powers. For play is in children mental, while with beasts it is the body alone that plays.

Playthings need not be rich ; the fancy supplies so much. The old doll is often the favourite. The author relates that his little girl, sitting beside him in his study, wrote for a long time with a pen dipped in air on ever-clean paper. (He took it as a satire on himself !) Those playthings are best which stimulate activity.   Sand, for instance, is excellent.   Play with equals in years is essential to bring out the child's governing power, his resistance, his forgiveness, generosity, gentleness.   Towards the parent and teacher the proper attitude is not any of these qualities, but obedience and faith.*

The earliest games should further the development of mind, for physical maturity advances as with strides, and without help; later ones should put the physical development upon a level with the mental, which advances too rapidly under influences of school and years. Let the little child toy, sing, look, listen; but the boy and girl run, climb, throw, build, get hot and cold. The most delightful game is *speaking*, first, of the child himself, later on, of the parents to him. You cannot talk too much to your children in play and for pleasure, nor too little in punishing and teaching.

---

* The Kindergarten system has embodied much that Richter says about the educative power of games. But in so far as Kindergarten games are under the direction of the teacher, it is obvious that they do not take the place of genuine playground games.

Chapter IV.

Children's Dances.

Dancing is the proper motion of a child. Children's balls are, however, most pernicious.

Spontaneous dancing to music is healthful and natural. . . . Music is an invisible dance, and dancing is a silent music. . . . In the child happiness *dances,* in the man, at most, it only smiles and weeps. . . . Running and climbing strengthen individual muscles, dancing exercises and equalises all the muscles, like a physical poetry. Further, the music connected with it imparts to the body and mind that material order which enfolds the highest, and regulates pulse-beats, steps, and thoughts.

Chapter V.

Music.

Music, the only fine art which men and all classes of beasts—spiders, mice, elephants, fishes, birds—have in common, must ceaselessly influence that combination of man and animal, the child. . . . It is probable that the first music heard, perhaps as an undying echo in the infant, forms the secret thorough-bass, the melodic theme of some future master of sound, who

will only vary it harmonically in his after-composi-
tions. . . . Music, rather than poetry, should be
called the "happy art." She imparts to children
nothing but heaven, for as yet they have not lost
one; and as yet no memories ring muffled peals for
them. . . . Choose melting strains and soft tones;
even with these you will only excite the child to frisk
about. . . . Of all musical instruments the one
most useful for educative purposes is the voice—the
instrument that the performer was born with. In the
childhood of nations speaking was singing. In song,
the man, the tone, and the heart become one, whilst
instruments only seem to lend him their voices. . . .
What is more beautiful than a merry singing child?
. . . Though the father of a family may seldom or
never sing, I would have him do it for his children,
and the mother for him and for them. . . .

Why should not harmony be employed as a soul-
medicine against the maladies of children—vexation,
obstinacy, anger?

Chapter VI.

Commands, Prohibitions, Punishments.

In regard to these matters our author confesses himself on the side of Basedow, and at
variance with Rousseau, who (like H. Spencer

in our day) would have a child rewarded and punished merely by physical consequences.

Parental will cannot, and ought not to assume the appearance of mere chance. Rousseau's whole system of education would waste a grown-up man on a growing one,* but life was not given that the educated may merely educate in turn.

The sense of freedom in a child comes before the feeling of necessity. He treats even inanimate things as willing agents; every event is an action, every obstacle an enemy. Endurance is taught by the spiritual necessity of a foreign will. Trust in man is taught by confidence in parent's words.

No pleasure is to be taken by parents in their own power of commanding and forbidding, but in the child's free action. The child is to be irresistibly bound by the parent's word, but the parent is not to be afraid to issue commands which, under altered conditions, he may see fit to reverse. Your lawgiving power may issue each day new decretals and pastoral letters. . . . Forbid by words, rather than by actions. Do not snatch the knife out of your child's hands, but let him lay it down himself at your desire. Guidance is to be preferred to pressure. . .

---

* Emile's tutor was to be at his side for twenty-five years in order to give time for consequences to reveal themselves.

Forbid the whole if it is difficult to separate the parts of an action. . . . Respect for property is to be exacted rigidly. The child is to be taught that he owes all to his parents.

In reproof, a child's ear readily distinguishes a decided from an angry tone.

And here follows a comparison between the father's and the mother's manner of saying " no ! " which is not in favour of the latter. He asks, " was there ever in history an instance of a woman training a dog ? " and his complaint is, that women (1) are too apt to speak in an angry tone, (2) use too many words in prohibiting, (3) are too ready to withdraw refusals. " *Pas trop gouverner* " is a good rule in education, as in politics.

Do not preach against faults that come with years, but only against those that increase with years.

Arts that come of themselves need not be taught in haste. On the other hand, capabilities, *e.g.* correct pronunciation, sense of order, require gradual cultivation.

It is a fault in us to consider every difference of a child from us as a failing.

You must not be everlastingly winding up your children nor your watches.

Forbid in a gentle voice, that a whole gamut of increased force may be open to you, and only once. This last rule costs labour; for in children, as in men, there is to be found a system of delay, which requires three words of command for every rapid determination.

The author recommends forbearance if the child ceases the forbidden act by degrees, and delay on the part of the parent in refusing and punishing, except in the case of very young children, where the punishment should have more of the character of physical effect. The fulfilment of parents' wishes, dependent solely on the love and free choice of the children, is as important as is obedience to commands. Obedience without consideration of motive is of no value, except to make things easier for the parents. It is a free agent that has to be trained, and the child, like its elders, would rather make presents than pay debts.

Chapter VII.

Punishment.

The very word is unchildlike. Punishment should
fall only upon a guilty conscience, and children, like
animals, have at first one void of offence. A child
that strikes should alone be struck, if possible, by the
object itself. . . . Never let a contest of parental
and childish obstinacy take place. After a certain
amount of exerted authority leave to the aggrieved
child the victory of " No " ; you may be certain he will
avoid such a galling one next time.

The tendency of children to conceal faulty
acts is here briefly sketched, and proper
treatment suggested. But the subject is
fully dealt with in a later chapter. Richter
much deprecates what he terms " after-
anger." When punishment has been inflicted, the time immediately succeeding is
of the utmost importance.

After the hour of storm, every seed-word finds a
softened warm ground; fear and hatred of the punishment, which at first hardened the soul and struggled
against the reproof, are now past, and gentle words
penetrate and heal, as honey relieves the sting of
a bee. In this hour one can say much if the mildest

voice is used, and if by the signs of one's own pain that of the sufferer is mitigated. But poisonous is the after-winter of after-anger; at the most an after-grief, not an after-torment, is allowable.

He accuses the mother of being especially liable to fall into this error. The effect of it is, either that the anger passes over the child who lives only in the present, and therefore does not willingly dwell on the past, or else that he is embittered, and learns to do without love.

An after-grief may, however, do much good when the child is at the age of thirteen or fourteen, if it consist of seriousness on the part of father or of mother, and of the withdrawal of the signs of love which at this age are thirsted for. Even these cannot be done without by a younger child.

In reproof one should never pass judgment on the nature. Never say, for instance, "You are a liar," but solely on the deed, as, "You have told a lie." The former is felt to be undeserved, and the child is more ready to feel the wrong-doing of others than his own. There is an inalienable sense of freedom which makes him feel, immediately after the wrong act, the power to do or to refrain. It is sinful to kill this sense, and for the same reason, positive marks of disgrace (dunce caps, etc.) are not good, though we may take away signs of honour and distinction which would be otherwise given as rewards.

Never let the least pain be inflicted scoffingly, but earnestly, oftener sorrowfully. The sorrow of the parents then purifies that of the child. For instance, when Fénélon's royal pupil indulged in ebullitions of passion, the bishop commanded all the servants to wait upon the king's son earnestly and silently, and to let silence preach.

In a later chapter on this subject of commands and obedience, the author says—

Raise up in the child by every possible means the conception of a higher tribunal than that of feeling. If he desire any forbidden thing do not move it further from him, but rather nearer to him, so that he may overcome that desire by a sense of duty. Place your command simply before him, without any attractive concomitants which may make it seem lighter than it is; by such delicate concealment of your rule, chance, which forms no habits, is made the master. The manner in which the command is obeyed is of infinitely more importance than the mere act of obedience. Neither veil a refusal, as mothers are too apt to do; perpetual concealments are impossible. Why will you not save yourself from them by a naked "no," and accustom your boy to cheerful resignation? Quie submission to arbitrariness weakens, but to necessity strengthens. Be then a fate to your child.

Chapter VIII.

Screaming and Crying.

Children are excitable and sensitive, affected by the weather and other circumstances, and in common with weak men they find it difficult to stop what they have begun.

Four causes of crying are enumerated, each of them requiring different treatment.

1. Outward hurts: compassion is here out of place; we should say "courage!" otherwise the sufferer will cry on for pleasure.

2. Illness: here the mother's gentle soothing voice is in its right place.

Spiritual regimen is however not to be intermitted on account of the illness of the body. In curing the latter you must not bring disease upon the mind. As Richter says, in a later chapter, "the sick are much better served by the mental excitement of pictures and games on the pillow, than by physical indulgence."

Think always only of the best, the good will soon come of itself.

3. Desire for something.

Here hold fast Rousseau's advice : never let the child gain an inch of ground by this war-cry.

It were better to give him something different rather than the thing he cries for.

4. Ill-temper on account of loss, vexation. This is not to be allowed to gain ground. Some occupation may be suitably prescribed to turn the attention.

Do not put to flight naughtinesses that fade with years, by those that grow with years. Children's tears dry up sooner than men's sighs begin.

Chapter IX.

The Trustfulness of Children.

Children understand the speech of others long before their own is developed. Trust is inherent, especially towards parents. All human intercourse pre-supposes confidence in the words of others : our knowledge of past times, of distant countries, of most of the sciences, is based on it.

But faith reveals its glorious form most richly when its object is moral. In the intellectual world there is more belief in what men say; in the moral, in what men are.

Lovers trust in each other, the friend in the friend, the noble heart in humanity, and the faithful in God. This is Peter's rock, the firm foundation of human worth. Nature has richly endowed children with receptivity. The bones of the ear in a child are as large as in an adult. This should be a clue to their power of trust.

Sacredly guard childlike trust, without which there could be no education.

Never forget that the little child looks to you as to a lofty genius and apostle, full of revelations, whose word he believes in implicitly, much more entirely than in his equals, and that an apostle's lie devastates a whole moral world. Bury your infallibility, then, neither under useless proofs, nor under confessions of error; admission of ignorance comports better with you. . . . Least of all support religion and morality by reasons; the multitude of pillars darken and narrow the churches. Let the holy in yourself—without lock and turn-key—be directed to the holy in the child.

Faith opens the little breast to the great old heart. To injure this faith is to resemble Calvin, who banished music out of the churches; for faith is the echo of the unearthly music of the spheres.

Here follows an appendix on physical education, which subject has been so ably worked out of late years that it seems hardly worth while to dwell on Richter's somewhat discursive argument in favour of a bracing regimen.

FOURTH FRAGMENT.

ON FEMALE EDUCATION.

THE author proposes to discuss (1) the education given usually by women; (2) their special vocation for this office as compared with men; (3) the education of girls as based on these considerations.

CHAPTER I.

The salvation of education can be brought to badly educated and educating states and to fathers immersed in business by mothers alone. . . .

Mothers have the disadvantage of being always with their children, so that they see faults constantly repeated, and also see each new leaf of development put forth; hence they tend to exaggerate in both cases. The physical care of her children to some extent deadens the mother to their mental culture.

The father, who (unless he is a country gentleman or a country clergyman) has little leisure for his children, must exercise the law-giving power of education, and the mother the administrative. . . .

Let the husband continue to be the lover of his wife, and she will readily listen to what he says about education, at least of the mind. In this way the husband may bestow care and attention on the first and most important education, that given by the mother, which no after schools, tutors, or paternal praise or blame can ever replace. . . .

The husband marks only full stops in a child's life, the wife, commas and semicolons. Mothers be fathers! we might cry, and fathers be mothers! for the two sexes complete each sex. The man works by exciting powers; the woman by maintaining order and harmony among them. . . . The soldier will educate warlikely, the poet poetically, the divine piously, the mother alone humanly.

Then follows an urgent appeal to mothers to make full use of their opportunities and privileges.

O women! be the mothers of your children! But you mothers who do not educate your children, how should your thanklessness for an unmerited blessing cause you to hang down your heads in shame before every childless mother, before every childless wife!

Richter here pays a tribute untranslatable

in its tenderness to the memory of his wife's gentle sister, who died longing vainly to press a child to her heart.

CHAPTER II.

The Nature of Girls.

The character of women determines the special education to be given them. The author notes—

Unbroken unity of nature, clear perception, and apprehension of the present, sharpness of wit, keen spirit of observation, ardour with repose, excitability and emotional sensibility, ready passage from inward to outward and *vice versa*, from gods to ribbons, from motes to solar-systems. . . . Nature has directly formed woman to be a mother.

CHAPTER III.

Girls should, therefore, be educated to be mothers, that is, teachers. . . . But before and after being a mother, a girl is a human being; neither motherly nor wifely destination can overbalance nor replace the human, but must become its means not its ends. As above the poet stands the artist, the hero, so above the mother, the human being; and as the artist forms

something higher than his work with his work—himself the creator of that work—so does the mother along
with the child form her own more holy self.

Though nature has ordained womanhood
for motherhood, we must not anticipate any
more than we need oppose the appointments
of nature in the education of women ; nature
works blindly to her ends ; education must
not oppose, but integrate.   Our object must
be to make the character complete by puri-
fying and toning down the preponderating
force by means of other harmonising powers.

Woman feels, but does not see herself ; she is all
heart, and her ears are ears of the heart.   What is to
be done ?   Feelings come and go, like light troops following the victory of the present ; ideas, like troops of
the line, are undisturbed and stand fast.   Shall we
now, by anatomising, rob the heart of its fair fulness
of inner life ?   It were sad if we could do it ; but Söm-
merung, after the thousand ears he had dissected, still
experienced the charm of harmony.

Let the girl learn to test, analyse, explain, not her
feeling, but the object of her feeling ; and then, when
she has herself found the error of the object, she will
be forced while the emotion lasts to follow only the
insight gained.   Do not attack feelings, but imagin-

ation. The latter brings together various possibilities
into one reality; but if this imaginary focus be dis-
persed by the concave lens of reason into its compo-
nent rays, then the feeling is not wasted, only better
placed.

Morbid sensibility is to be checked, especially when excited by merely imaginary
griefs.

Real life-sorrows sometimes find such hearts cal-
lous. . . . Feelings, flowers, and butterflies, live all
the longer the later they are developed. . . .

The cultivation of so-called accomplish-
ments merely for display, is spoken of as a
sin not only against the girl herself but
against the Spirit of God.

To recommend any excellence she may possess, be it
art or knowledge or the sanctuary of the heart, as a
bait to catch a husband, is to shoot wild fowl with
diamonds, or to knock down fruit with a sceptre.

Wilfulness, foolish fears, affectation, these
are girlish faults. Fears, as of spiders, mice,
and the like, are to be overcome by the exhibition of the beauty of the parts and limbs

of the creature which excites no admiration as a whole.

Richter is strongly in favour of home-education for girls. Girls, he thinks, are more influenced by example, especially bad example, than boys.

Girls depend on one heart, boys on many heads. . . . The most that a girl could find in a school would be a second mother, the father would be wanting, and men's companionship, that of father, brothers, parents' friends, is essential to the education of the girl.*

Again, the moral instruction in school is necessarily too didactic ; while in the home it is received as the natural unobtrusive accompaniment of the thread of life. Yet all these evils, he allows, are less likely to be produced by day-schools than by boarding-schools. With respect to subjects of instruction, he would have the powers of attention, of judging, of observation, cultivated by sciences, such as botany, astronomy ; reason-

---

* A similar argument would apply to boys' schools, *i.e.* that they have not enough women's companionship.

ableness by mathematics, especially geometry; interest in the larger concerns of human life by reading travels and voyages, the history of great men and great events. Music is also to be learnt, and one foreign language. In the following chapter he says :—

> Music, if only listened to and not scientifically cultivated, gives too much play to the feelings and fancy ; the difficulties of the art draw forth the whole energies of the soul. Hence thorough-bass should be taught to girls. . . .
>
> Sewing and knitting are to be considered as recreation rather than work, and they do not preclude the dangerous habit of day-dreaming, which, in fact, is best attacked by the details of housekeeping.*

Merriment is to be cultivated and allowed free play among the girls.

> Sorrow causes more absence of mind and confusion than so-called levity. Never fear that feminine merriment precludes depth of soul and feeling. Does it so in men ? And did not the lawgiver Lycurgus and his

---

* Richter wrote, it must be remembered, before the system of large day-schools for girls had been fairly tried. His testimony in favour of a thoroughly intellectual education for girls is the most valuable part of the chapter.

Spartans in every place build an altar in the house to Laughter? It is precisely under external cheerfulness that the quiet powers of the heart increase and grow to their full stature.

Mothers are recommended to assist their girls to become externally French, internally German, " to convert life into a comic poem, which surrounds its deep meaning with merry forms."

It may be questioned whether any special education is needed for women of genius. The author decides in the negative, for—

Talent, not genius, can be repressed, just as a chemical compound can be destroyed, but not a single element.

Yet, if a man of genius must also be a man and a citizen, and if possible a father, a woman must not think herself elevated by her genius above her appointed day-labour in life. If a Jean-Jacques * writes upon education, a clever Johanna-Jacquelina need not be ashamed of putting his precepts into practice. On the contrary the rare excess of female genius should be rather an additional call to the work than a passport for neglecting it. But if such a woman is ever ashamed of deeds, while priding herself on ideas, thene inded

---

* Rousseau.

will her destiny avenge itself. . . . But if she unite her woman's calling with genius, a mighty and rare blessedness will fill her heart. The clouds which pour their floods on the valleys, gently dissolve on the heights.

CHAPTER IV.

On the education of a princess, in the form of private instructions of a prince to the governess of his daughter.

This chapter is a satirical appendix to what Richter has already said about the education of girls. It is somewhat more difficult than usual to disentangle his jest from his earnest. He is at any rate in earnest when he recommends that the princess's sound common sense should be cultivated, and that she should be encouraged in her love of seeing some work, *e.g.* a picture, grow under her hands. If, in her marriage, she is to expect less happiness, because less freedom of choice than falls to the lot of the average woman, she may at least open to herself a never-failing spring by cultivating early the " mother's heart."

FIFTH FRAGMENT.

EDUCATION OF A PRINCE.

THE subject of this, as of the last chapter, is necessarily of less general interest than the rest of the work. The special duties and difficulties of the tutor's task are dwelt upon in the author's forcible way.

Men of the world bring their influence to bear even upon the early period of the prince's life. If anything sets itself in opposition to the great earnestness of a prince's tutor, indeed of any teacher, it is the worldly views of worldly people, even the most honourable and impartial. If the pupil has to be conducted through two totally different worlds, out of the one into the other, out of that really great world in which nobility of soul, character, great principles, and comprehensive views alone were valued,—where only despisers of the passing hour and men of eternity stood,—where an Epaminondas, a Socrates, a Cato, still spoke from their tombs, and delivered oracles as from an everlasting

44

Delphic cavern,—where earnestness of purpose, and Man, and God, outweighed all else,—out of this into the world of sham greatness, in which all that is great and departed is little esteemed, and what is trifling and present is alone held important,—where everything is custom and nothing is duty, not to mention kingly. duty,—where the whole country is perhaps looked upon as an estate, all offices as appendages of the crown,— where inspiration seems a passing love affair, or a mere artistic talent,—if all these counter-influences are to be brought to bear upon the royal pupil, must not the tutor's influence be almost submerged? . . .

The chief means of obviating the difficulties is to teach the prince the dignity of his position, because he alone adorns his station who believes himself to be adorned by it. As your pupil can never think too modestly of himself, so can he never think too proudly of his office ; the reverse of this produces misery every-where. His office—a high priesthood at the altar of the State—demands from a fallible human being the powerful agency of a God. He is not merely the first servant of the State, but its very heart, which alter-nately receives and sends out its life-blood ; he is its centre of gravity, which gives direction to its varied forces. Then let German philosophy show him some-thing different from the ignoble conclusions of French philosophy and of worldliness. Verily the ancient error of regarding princes as the ambassadors and anointed of God (which, in fact, all men are, only in different degrees) is much nobler and more efficacious for good than the modern error of regarding them only as the agents of selfish extortions, that is, of the devil!

Richter analyses carefully the motives that tempt princes to declare war, and would have the royal pupil taught that the people alone should decide upon its necessity, since it is they who reap the bitter fruits of it.

The reading of history is to be the antidote to the love of martial glory.

History alone shows how little mere bravery appertains to glory, for a cowardly nation is more rare upon the earth than a brave man. What nation in ancient or modern times is not brave? The lower Rome's free spirit sank, the more wildly and more vehemently rose the merely brave spirit. . . .

The frequent arming of the ancient slaves, as of the modern beggars, testifies against the value of the common bravery of fists and wounds. . . .

But the truly, because freely, brave nation carries on its war of freedom at home, against every hand that would stay its flight or blind its eye. This is indeed the longest and bravest war, and the only one that admits of no truce. Just so brave, and in a higher sense, may a monarch be. . . .

Let the great ideal of art, greatness in repose, be the ideal of the throne.

The chapter concludes with four aphorisms.

To form a brave man, educate boldly.

Not without reason do the fairest flowers borrow their names from princes. Power cannot have too gentle an expression.

He who mistrusts humanity is quite as often deceived as he who trusts men.

Tutor! have at heart no work of your pupil so much as his love of work!

SIXTH FRAGMENT.

MORAL EDUCATION OF BOYS.

CHAPTER I.

HONOUR, honesty, firm will, steadiness, courage against threatened dangers, fortitude, openness, self-respect, just self-esteem, contempt for the world's opinion, uprightness, and perseverance,—all these and like words delineate only one-half of the moral nature, namely, moral strength and dignity. The second half embraces all that concerns our outward life, the realm of love, gentleness, benevolence,—we may term it moral beauty. Though the former seems to turn inwards to one's own personality, the latter outwards to that of others, though the one appears a repelling, the other an attracting pole, and though the one holds sacred an idea, the other a life,—yet both claim supremacy over the self whose rule is alone acknowledged by the desires and the sins against the twin stars of the heart, for honour as well as love makes a sacrifice of selfishness. . . . On true moral strength hangs love, as the

48

sweetest fruit on the thickest bough; weakness, like Vesuvius, trembles only to devastate.

Pure love not simply *can* do everything, she *is* everything.

One age requires men in order to come into existence, another in order to continue to exist; ours requires them for both reasons; yet our education fears nothing so much as making boys manly, and it unmans them when it can. Nurseries and schoolrooms are become the sacristies of those temples which the Romans built to their deities Pavor and Pallor. As though the world were too full of courage, teachers engraft fear by their punishments and their actions; courage is only recommended by words. Letting alone, not enterprise, is crowned.

The ancients, in their desire for strength, forgot benevolence,—we err in the contrary direction. Teachers at any rate have the excuse, though a delusive one, that childish courage, unbalanced by prudence, easily turns to rashness, and attacks teacher and fate. But we must remember that years increase light, but not strength, and that we more easily provide life's pilgrim with a guide than restore to him the legs and wings that we have cut off lest he should run or fly away. Like soldiers, we ought to begin with common courage, and proceed upwards to honour.

Injunctions of an earlier chapter against exciting children's fears are repeated in greater detail, and the importance of encouraging a healthy cheerfulness is enforced both with respect to anticipated and actual pains.

Courage does not consist in blindly overlooking danger, but in meeting it with the eyes open. Do not attempt, therefore, to make boys brave by saying, " It will not hurt you,"—for in that case the sheep would fight as bravely as the lion,—but by the better saying, " What does it matter ? only a hurt ! " For you may safely reckon on something in every human breast which no wounds can reach, on a firm celestial axis amidst unstable earthly axes, insomuch as man, unlike the beasts, has something more than pain to dread. . . .

Permit me to add a few ingredients to the tonic medicine of manliness before I pass to the most spiritual means of strengthening it. What, from the Fakeer to the martyrs, *i.e.* of Christianity, of love, of parental affection, and even of liberty, has conquered the body, opinion, desire, the rack ? Has it not always been an idea rooted in the heart ? Give the boy, then, some one living idea, then he will be capable of becoming a man.

Every boy pictures to himself some condition, some trade, as the work-house and sorrow-house of life, and some other, usually his father's, as a Belvidere of Hope. Take from him these delusive charts of heaven and hell, which make him the prisoner of fear and desire.

Bring him, but not by dead hearsay,—by living experience,—into acquaintanceship with the joys of the
most diverse conditions. It is much more important
that the child should not weakly dread and avoid
any gloomy condition than that he should not desire
and strive after a brilliant one.

Above all, the chief ingredient in this
"tonic medicine" is to be the consideration
of the future in its true aspect, namely as a
scene of activity, not of self-pleasing.

No science has so many teachers as the science of
happiness or of pleasure; as if this had not already
planted its pulpit in the hearts of cats, vultures, and
other beasts. Will you, then, teach what the beasts
know? . . . If you seek to inspire reverence
for pure worth, justice, and religion, by any other
means than by exhibiting the simple forms of these
children of God,—if it were only by showing some
advantage to the animal propensities derivable there-
from, instead of teaching that all pleasures are due
sacrifices to these divinities, then have you sullied the
pure spirit and made it petty and hypocritical. If life
is a battle, let the teacher be a poet who shall animate
the boy to meet it with needful songs; and hence accustom him to regard his future not as the path from
pleasures to other pleasures, however innocent, nor
even as a gleaning, a harvest of fruits after the present

spring-time, but as a time in which he must execute some life-long plan. In short, let him aim at a long course of activity, not of enjoyment.

In London it is he who was born rich, not he who is becoming so, that commits suicide; and, on the other hand, it is not the poor man that kills himself, but he who is becoming so. The miser grows old enjoying rather than wearied of life, whilst the heir who comes into possession of the wealth he had collected sinks into *ennui.*

I would rather be the court gardener who watches and protects an aloe for fifteen years, until at last it opens to him the heaven of its blossom, than the prince who is hastily called to look on the opened heaven.

The true source of power is suggested.

If man resemble iron in his strength, in the inflammability of his passions he resembles that metal in combination with sulphur, at whose touch the hot bar of iron falls down in drops. Does mere passion give strength? as certainly as a Parisian Revolution, freedom, or as comets, brilliantly lighted nights!

Admit your boy as much as possible into the Stoic School, less by instruction than by the examples of the genuine Stoics of all times. In order that he may not mistake the Stoic for a Dutchman, or for a stupid savage, let him see that the true inner fire of the heart glows in those men who through their whole life manifest a steadfast will, and have not, like the passionate, isolated wishes and desires; and name to him such men as Socrates and Cato, who were animated by a constant, and therefore tranquil, inspiration. This steadfast will, which controls every inward tumult, does not pre-suppose any single aim, but the grand final aim of life, which is the central sun of all orbits. It can therefore produce only a strong or great life, not merely a single great or strong deed,—of which every weakling is capable,—just as a mountain does not consist of an isolated peak, but of a connected system of earth-masses.

A steadfast volition can aim only at the most general, the Divine,—whether freedom, or science, or art, or religion; the more special the volition is, the oftener it is disturbed in its aims by the outer world. This ideal is not to be communicated by education,—for it is the very inmost self,—but it is to be pre-supposed by every educator, and hence to be called into life. Life is kindled only by life; and hence the highest in the child only by example, either of those living or of the great dead, or (which unites both influences) by poetry itself.

Much that is very plausible and very prolix will be urged against this idealisation of youth by pedagogic elephant hunters, who hunt what is great in order to have it tame, serviceable, and toothless in their stables. They will say: "All this is very fine, but only fit for the world of romance. What can come of such ex-cessive straining upwards of the youthful mind but senseless contemplation and opposition to the real world in which he must live? In short, the young man has to go forth into the world and the times as the old man has done, and to forget his empty castles in the air. Those ideal notions are only of value so far as they exhibit useful reality; therefore in a truly allegorical sense, in Zurich every professor, whether of law, divinity, etc., must be enrolled in a guild of shoemakers, weavers, or some other trade—and only thus can they serve their country!"

This last proposition I admit. But heavens! would you then send unarmed into the field of battle that which the world and time would weaken in any case? And will you act just as if from later years gradual elevation of the baseness of life was to be expected instead of further depression? Ought you not to treat the eyes of the mind at least as carefully as those of the body, before which you place first the concave spectacles which diminish slightly, because their use necessitates later on those which diminish more? The worst you have to dread is that the youth shall exalt some reality into his ideal; but worse will be the result of your efforts namely, that he should darken and materialise his ideal with the real. Alas! that happens well enough without you; the ripe sunflower no longer turns its heavy seed-laden head to the sun. The Rhine soon finds its way to the plain through which it creeps with no glittering waterfall. What is all the gain which the young soul can win from the avoidance of a few false steps and views, compared with the tremendous loss of the holy fire of youth, if he must creep into the cold narrow life without wings, without great plans, in short, as nakedly as most people creep out of it? How shall life ripen without the ideal glow of youth, or the vine without August? The fairest deeds of men, although in their coldest time of life, sprang from late-appearing seeds which the Tree of Life of their childhood's paradise has borne.

Have you never seen how a man may be governed through his whole life by one divine image of his spring-time?

With what else than the bread-cart of clever selfishness would you replace this guiding pole-star?

Finally, what is the one thing needful to man? Truly not the strength to sacrifice all for the best; for let a god once appear in reality, and man divests himself of all that is human that the deity does not need. But he needs something more than strength,—faith and reverence for a divinity who requires sacrifices of a better kind. All men would be gods under the leadership of a god. But blot the ideal out of the breast, then vanish with it temple, altar, and all!

CHAPTER II.

Truthfulness.

Truthfulness,—I mean intentional and self-sacrificing truth-speaking,—is less a branch than a blossom of a man's moral strength. Weaklings must lie, hate it as they may. One threatening look drives them into the midst of a net of sins. The difference between the Middle Age and the Present consists less in the existence of crime, cruelty, and lust,—for these, especially the last, were abundant enough before the discovery of America,—than in the want of truthfulness. Men say no longer : " Ein Wort, ein Mann " (a word, a man, *i.e.* it is sufficient for a *man* to say a thing), because we are obliged to say : " Ein Mann (ist nur) ein Wort " (a man is only a word).

The first sin on the earth—fortunately the devil committed it on the Tree of Knowledge—was a lie ; and the last will surely be a lie too ; for the world does penance for the increase in truths by the decrease in truthfulness.

Lying, the devouring lip-cancer of the inner man, is more sharply punished and defined by the feeling of nations than by philosophers. The Greeks, who permitted their gods to do as much with impunity as their modern representatives the gods of the earth allow themselves, condemned them for a perjury—that quintessence of a lie—to remain for a year lifeless underground in Tartarus, and to suffer nine years of torment. The ancient Persians taught their children nothing of morality except truthfulness.

Auton tells us that to "lie" and to "lie" (down) are from the same root ; probably the word has reference to the abject slave who dared raise neither body nor spirit. Lying and stealing, and a box on the ear, which the ancient Germans avoided more than a wound, are brought together in their proverbs. . . . The German tourney was closed to the liar as well as to the murderer. I grant that in the case of the greatest tournament, war, the greatest duplicity opens the lists for knightly exercise to a prince with whom no treaty nor peace is to be made.

Is this hatred of false words founded on violation of mutual right and confidence, or upon the injury consequent upon broken compacts? That this is not the explanation is shown by another fact, that we much more readily pardon and even choose lying action than lying speech. Action, silence, gesture, more often lie than the tongue, which a man guards as long as he can from the hideous perpetration of a lie, as a disease of the inner man. Are we not accustomed already, without knowing it, to innumerable fictions of the law—to political secret articles, to false hair, teeth, calves,— without being any the less shocked when a man pronounces a deliberate lie? What deceptions everywhere, from London (otherwise so lie-hating, where yet three-fourths of the money is false *) to Pekin, where wooden hams bound up in pig's skin are exposed for sale! If a distinguished warrior or courtier is less ashamed of a fraud or of a bankruptcy than of a lie, at the reproach of which he will shoot or stab

---

* In 1806.

himself; and if worldly men, even moralists, will commit themselves to a lying ambiguity of action rather than to a decided lie; if no blush is so burning as that at the sin of lying, must then word be something higher than deed, the tongue be more than the hand? The question is not to be answered altogether by referring to the ambiguity of action as compared with the simplicity of speech, since deeds are not always ambiguous, and since men pause more frequently before acting than before speaking. People are not ashamed of slandering and undermining the fortune of another while they would not speak a lie to his face.

What makes it so unholy? It is this: two individuals are separated from one another as upon islands, and imprisoned behind the bars of bone and the curtains of the skin. Mere movement shows the one only that the other is alive, it does not show his soul. Even the animated eye often speaks as well out of one of Raphael's Madonnas, which houses no soul; and the cabinet of wax figures is hollow, and the ape dumb. By what glorified body does the individuality of the man become visible? Merely through language, this expressed reason, this audible freedom. I speak of the universal inborn language, without which every particular language, as species of it, would be neither intelligible nor possible. Whilst instinct and machines imitate all the other signs of life, in this alone does the freedom of one creator of thought make itself known to another, and this herald of freedom announces indi-

viduals to each other like princes. . . . Only by
our present conversion of mobile speech into immobile
writing or painting has the blackness of the lie become
diminished, for when everything is only a symbol,
every sign can be symbolised to infinity.

Suppose, however, a fellow-man steps forward and
tells me a plain lie. How annihilating! His true
self has fled from me, only the fleshly image remains;
whatever the latter may say is as meaningless as the
wind, which with all its howling expresses no pain.
A word effaces or often explains an act, but seldom is
the reverse the case; and only a series of acts takes
away the sting from a word. The whole fairy-palace
of a man's thoughts becomes invisible to me at the
sound of one lie which is the mother of many. How
could I hold converse with one who carried about
a talking-machine with him, whilst he had other
thoughts than those which were pumped out of the
machine? More than that, he gives me—an unquali-
fied injury—a machine in return for my inner self,
errors in exchange for my truths, and breaks down the
spiritual bridge between us, or makes it into a draw-
bridge which he lets down for himself, but draws up
when others would cross it.

Now let us return to the dear children.

During the first five years they speak neither truth
nor falsehood, they only talk, and their talking is a
thinking aloud; but since one half of their thought is
a "yes," the other half a "no," and, unlike ourselves,

both escape them, they seem to lie whilst they are
merely talking to themselves. Further: they like to
play in early years with the newly acquired art of
talking; thus they often talk nonsense in order to
listen to their own babble. Often they do not understand some word in your question (*e.g.* the little ones
confuse "to-day," "to-morrow," numbers, degrees
of comparison) and give rather a mistaken than a
lying answer. Above all they use their tongues more
in play than in earnest, *e.g.* to their dolls and playthings (just as a minister or historian attributes long
speeches to his puppets), so that this play-talk is easily
employed towards living men. Again, children readily
fly to the sunny side of hope; they say if the bird or
dog has escaped, without further reason, "it will soon
come back." But since they cannot altogether dis-
tinguish hopes, that is, fancies, from recollections or
truths, their self-deception assumes the form of a lie.
Thus, an otherwise truthful little girl used frequently
to describe to me apparitions of the Christ-child * and
to relate what He had said and done. It is a question
whether children do not often relate remembered
dreams, which they no doubt confuse with tales they
have heard. Connected with this tendency is the
teasing talk of boys at eight or nine years, a mode
in which their superabundant energy finds vent.

---

* Supposed by German children to bring their Christ-
mas gifts.

In all these cases when the time has not come for holding before the child the dark mirror which shall reveal the true form of the lie, all that we need say is "be serious, do not talk nonsense."

Lastly, we must on no account confuse an untruth concerning future matters with one concerning the past. If in the case of an adult we do not place a breach of contract which has reference to the future on a par with a black perjury concerning the past, still further asunder ought to be placed children's breaches of promise from their untruthfulness as to facts; for to their view time, like space, extends itself indefinitely, and a day is as inscrutable as a year.

Something quite different, and worse, is a narrative lie, by which the teller would gain something in the future.

Truthfulness involving even bloody sacrifices for a word as such, is a divine blossom on earthly roots; hence it is not the virtue first in time, but the last. The simple savage is full of deceit, both in word and deed; the peasant is tempted by the smallest danger to lie about the past: though he will keep his word. Nevertheless, people demand from a child whose education has still to be given him the last and finest fruit of it. How mistaken you are, you may see from this fact that lying children become truthful men (otherwise all would be alike); I appeal to the experience of every conscience. Meanwhile, two kinds of children's lying are to be distinguished by the motives prompting them ; namely, deceitful acts and words arising from the desire to gain something, and secondly, the abjuration of their own acts from fear of the consequences.

What is to be done in both cases ?

Rather, what is to be done before they arise ? That is the question.

The child, dazzled by the hot splendour of his individuality, which imprisons him, makes the first acquaintance with morality only in the person of another, and he recognises the ugliness of a heard lie before that of a spoken one. Show him then the throne of others' truth beside the abyss of others' falsehood; be what you command him to be, and often repeat that you will do even indifferent things because you have promised them. It will have a powerful effect upon the little heart, if his father whom he looks upon as a sort of free universal monarch is heard by him sometimes to complain that he must do something he is disinclined to do, because he has promised it. If the child has promised anything, remind him of it frequently as the time approaches, but say nothing more than " you said so," and urge him to it at last. But if he has committed a fault, your questions about it, so painful to him, cannot spare him sufficiently. The younger he is, the less you should question, the more you should appear all-knowing, or remain ignorant.

Do you not consider that you put your children to a fiery trial which a Huss and other martyrs have endured, when you put such small beings in the dilemma of obeying either their instinct of self-defence or an ideal, while you hold out the prospect of the rack after confession? For to them a displeased father is a torturing judge, a prince, and a fate; the rod of his anger is Jupiter's club, the next moment a torment, an eternity of hell-punishment.

To truth belongs freedom, at any rate to early truthfulness. The more freedom in the education, the truer the child; thus were all truth-loving nations and times, from the German to the British, free nations and times; lying China is a prison, and to "romance" meant to lie when the Romans were slaves.

If you must enquire, use affectionate words, not threats. . . .

In an earlier chapter (that on Punishments), Richter suggests that enquiries should be directed to the incidents connected with the child's act, as he is less likely to be prepared with a falsehood concerning them.

Thus, if you suspect a child has been on the ice, for instance, contrary to order, you might begin by asking him how long he was there, or who was with him. Thus he would be saved the temptation of denying the actual fact, and his penitence would be concentrated on the wrong deed to be confessed.* But if a lie has escaped the lips of the child and been brought home to him, then pronounce the judgment "guilty," that is, of "lying," with astonished tone and look, with the greatest horror at this sin against nature and against the Holy Ghost, and inflict the penalty.

For lying alone would I permit punishments that affect the honour, which must be as solemnly and completely removed as they have been imposed, in order not to habituate the offender to the disgrace by your diminishing it gradually. The Iroquois blacken the faces of those who sing false praises of a hero. The Siamese sew together the lips of lying women, as though they would be wounds if open. I have nothing to say against the blackening, I myself have sometimes punished lying—somewhat severely perhaps—by placing an ink-spot on the forehead, that was not to be washed out without permission, and which ate deeply into the conscience; but I think more highly of the Siamese plan of barring the lips, namely, forbidding to speak when speaking has been evil. . . . I believe this punishment is more just and decisive than the one which Rousseau and Kant would

---

* The translator has frequently put this advice to the test of experience, and found it invaluable. Children cannot easily be made sorry for two faults at once. Besides, the lie once uttered is a shield against the darts of penitence for the original fault.

inflict on a lying child, namely, not to believe him for a time, which would mean to seem not to believe him. In this case the judge would himself have to lie, whilst punishing lying; and will not the little culprit arrive at the knowledge of it, by his own consciousness of speaking truly?

And where and how will you make and give a reason for the some time necessary return from unbelief to belief? Kant's punishment, however, may sometimes be applied with advantage to grown-up daughters.

Do not command any child in his first six years to be silent about anything, even about a pleasure that you are preparing for one you love; nothing must shut in the open sky of children's frankness, not even the dawn of shame; to your secrets they will soon learn to add their own. The heroic virtue of silence requires for its practice the power of ripening reason; reason alone teaches silence, the heart teaches to speak. . . .

Do not despise small helps. For instance, do not force from the child a rapid answer to any question; haste will easily bring out a lie which he will seek to support by another. Give him a little time for thought before he answers. Further, in your most indifferent promises and assertions,—just because they are indifferent to you,—remember that children have a better memory than you, and especially for and against you; and that you must spare them every dangerous appearance of guilty or hasty untruthfulness.

The author has sometimes asked himself, whether

F

the sense of truth in children may not be injured by games of charades and children's comedies. For charades it may be said that they are only a continuation and higher imitation of the games with puppets and dolls and with one another, in which the children extemporised without sacrifice of truthfulness, as if they would take refuge behind the life of imitation from the raw atmosphere of reality. In charades the child is at once poet and actor, he lives indeed in a foreign character, but at the same time his language is unborrowed, being the product of the moment's warmth. In plays he learns to simulate the character coldly, and learns the speeches by heart with a view to an after-simulation of warmth in representing both. The charade has also the advantage of favouring originality since the answers are not learnt beforehand as in the case of the comedy. And since even great actors consider the expression of pure universal human nature, apart from artistic effect, as a matter of prime importance, children may surely be spared an exercise in which the gain is more doubtful than the loss.

Lastly, since truthfulness, when consciously involving self-sacrifice, is the blossom, or rather the fragrance of the blossom, of the whole moral growth, we must expect it to unfold with and upon the latter.

We have merely to root up the weeds whilst we give liberty for the character to grow, guarding against overpowering temptations, and forbidding soul-crippling formalities, such as children's returning thanks for a whipping, compliments to strangers, and the like.

CHAPTER III.

Training in Love.

Our author, following out his plan of carefully filling in the outlines, sketched with such a masterly hand in the opening chapters, repeats with fresh illustrations much that he has already said about the importance of the two forces of Love and Religion.

Love is an innate power of the heart, but differently apportioned; there are cold-blooded and warm-blooded souls, as there are animals. Many are born "knights of the love of their neighbour," * like Montaigne; many are armed neutrals towards their fellows. But this force, whether present as a sacred burning bush, or as a tinder-spark, has to be cared for in two ways in education, by protecting and by unfolding it.

The child begins with self-love, which offends us as little as an animal's, because its individuality as yet wrapped up in and blinded by its needs cannot feel its way to a second being, but the world of self is all in all.

Consequently the child finds nothing outside of it

---

* The order to which I allude was founded by the Consort of Charles III. of Spain.

lifeless, any more than itself, it projects its own soul into everything as the soul of the universe. A two-year old girl used to personify everything; for instance, "the door (which was opening) wants to go out;" "I will kiss my hand to the spring." This habit of attributing life to the lifeless, peculiar to children, furnishes an additional reason for our preventing them from treating lifeless things in a hostile manner.

At the same time love, with children as with animals, is already present as an impulse, and this central fire often breaks through the crust in the form of compassion, though not always. A child is sometimes not merely cold to the pains of animals and strangers, but even towards those of his relations and friends. Innocent children often take pleasure in putting themselves in the place of judgment where another is to be punished. Later on it may be noticed that boys approaching manhood evince the utmost love of teasing, selfishness and coldness of heart, as the night is coldest just before sunrise.

But the sun comes and warms the world, fulness of strength overflows into love, the full-grown stem encloses and nourishes the pith, the mischievous lad becomes a loving youth. Consequently you have not so much to engraft the buds of love, as to clear away the briars and moss of self that obstruct the sunlight. Everyone likes to love, if only he is permitted. Wherever a pulse beats, a heart is to be found within;

wherever there is any impulse towards love, behind it is love itself.

Children are to be taught the love of man by love of their neighbours in a literal sense. Parents are warned against, (1) passing harsh judgments upon their neighbours or their townsfolk before children ; (2) saying that other people's children are badly brought up; (3) speaking harshly of those who do wrong. The deed, not the doer, should be condemned. Conversely, it is well to praise the good deed, and not the child.

Having discussed means of fostering the power of love by giving it room to develope, the author turns to more direct means of calling it forth.

Bring before the child others' life and individuality in a living way, and he will love, because man is naturally so good that the devil has as it were only put a black frame round the divine image. The trunk of self nourishes with the same sap both its own fruit-buds and those of engrafted branches.

The cultivation of genuine sympathy with

others' lives, and of reverence for all life are discussed in turn.

Individuals and even nations often die without having ever once imagined themselves in any other position than their own.

Respect for animal-life and love of animals are recognised as aids in the development of the love of mankind.

The wonder and mystery of animal forms is to be dwelt upon. Fear of certain animals is to be overcome by the exhibition of the beauty and adaptation of their organs, so that interest in and admiration of the parts, may supersede terror at the whole.

Leibnitz replaced an insect that he had been long watching, on its leaf uninjured : let this be a command for the child. The Stoic school decided that he who killed a cock without occasion for it would be likely to ruin his father; and the Egyptian priest held it a desecration to kill an animal except as a sacrifice. In this lies the whole principle of reverence for life. All slaughter of animals should be only of necessity, as a sacrifice, or accidentally, hastily, involuntarily, or in self-defence. Hence if a child has been long watching an animal, as for instance a frog—its breathing, its leaps, its mode of life,—this animal, hitherto indifferent, has been transformed into pure life, in killing it you destroy the child's reverence for life. Thus, also, a domestic animal, or one to which the child is accustomed, should never be slaughtered before his eyes. . . . Even flowers should not be plucked ruthlessly and without purpose. . . .

Love of animals, like a mother's love for her children, has this excellence, that it arises without any expectation of return, still less of selfish advantage, and also this, that it finds at every moment an object and occasion for exercise.

The third source of love is love for love. Parents must awaken love by showing love, not frequent embraces and displays of affection which leave children cold and unimpressed, but loving words and looks.

Children are to be encouraged to perform little acts in order to learn to love, for in children the act awakens the impulse as in men the impulse leads to the act. But external signs of love are never to be commanded to children, for these are not, like deeds, causes, but only effects. Lastly, you parents, teach to love, and you will need no ten commandments. Teach to love, I say, that is, love.

Chapter IV.

Is an appendix to the discussion of Moral Education, and once more urges upon parents the importance of Religion, or rather of religious principle, as the basis of all moral worth.

Wise advice follows on many points connected therewith, such as the conservation of moral purity in children, especially in boys. Parents are cautioned against the common habit of evading their responsibilities when questioned by their children concerning the mysteries of life, and of leaving them to seek the gratification of their curiosity from the lips of coarse-minded companions or domestics.

Richter, in his treatment of this subject, anticipates much that has been written of late years,* we may therefore pass on to the—

---

* See Perez, "First Three Years of Childhood." Dr. E. Blackwell's "Counsel to Parents on the Moral Education of their Children," and others.

SEVENTH FRAGMENT.

WE pass now from the moral to the intellectual aspect of education. The heading of this portion of the work is suggestive—

Development of the Mental Conceptive-Power.

We have no English equivalent for Richter's " Bildungtrieb," but by the use of it he claims for the mind a power or tendency to produce new forms out of material already supplied, namely, ideas, which are worked up into new ideas by the mind itself. The power corresponds therefore in the main to what modern psychologists call Conception, but the word also implies an active impulse to be encouraged and developed.

The majority of teachers before Pestalozzi proposed only to pour in as much knowledge as possible, of every kind. Crippled pretenders they, to universal knowledge! always in process of being formed, and never forming anything for themselves; heirs of all ideas but leaving no inheritance behind them; they are specimens of such a mode of education but no proofs of its excellence!

We will proceed in a straight line to the central principle, instead of wandering about the circumference of the circle.

The faculty to be trained is then contrasted with the will—the source of all mental activity—whilst it is shown, at the same time, to be dependent upon volition. "The will," Richter says, " reproduces itself only; for the external action is as little the fresh product of the particular volition, as the word spoken is of the particular thought." That is, just as a word is not invented by the speaker to express his thought, but is the outcome of a growth of ages, as philologists show us, so is an act of ours the outcome of a whole series of thoughts and feelings interacting upon the volition that seems to us to give rise to it. On the other hand, the form of intellectual activity which he is

discussing, enlarges its world with new crea-
tions ; and, therefore, deserves, and is capable of direct cultivation on the part of the
educator, whilst the will can only be developed indirectly.

The mental power of conception which, in a higher
sense than the physical, works in accordance with the
will, is the distinguishing mark of man. No volition
conditions the series of mental images in an animal ;
while in our waking life we are always actively thinking, it is only in our dreams that we may be said to
receive thoughts. In a man of genius the forming of
ideas has the appearance of creation, in ordinary men
it appears merely necessary and the result of medita-
tion ; the difference is however really slight.

The stages of mental development are as follows :
(1) Language ; (2) Attention ; both of which should
place an idea more distinctly before the mind by de-
finition and close observation ; (3) Imagination or
mental representation, which is able to hold firmly a
chain of ideas in order that out of it the quantity
sought for, but as yet unknown, may leap forth as
a part, result, cause, symbol or image ; (4) Wit ; (5)
Reflection ; (6) Recollection.

From this almost genealogical gradation it will be
readily perceived that subjects of instruction fall into
two classes, of which one furnishes organic material to

the conceptive power—for instance, mathematics—the other, only dead material—for instance, descriptions of nature, of events, of customs. The old division into knowledge of words and knowledge of things is right in principle, but the catalogues usually given are fallacious. Thus languages come under the head of knowledge about words, history of nature and of nations, knowledge about things, instead of reversing the order.* Here one word about the misuse or excessive use of Natural History.

The author found to his delight that Goethe agreed with him in a thought which he had set down in his Commonplace-book in 1808. "What more educative power has the study of foreign animals than of any casual monster?" At most it is but honey on the nourishing bread. On the contrary native animals deserve the most exact description and life-sized illustrations. Truly how much a study of native plants and minerals would outweigh the small advantage to be

---

* Richter means that words are truly *things* with a history of their own; and Max Müller and others have shown that they can be studied scientifically. Teachers are beginning to see that this whole question turns upon the mode in which the knowledge is presented to the pupil's mind. One teacher may make Natural History or Latin, or even Mathematics into "dead material," while another may render it truly "organic," that is, supply food which the pupil can truly digest.

gained from the study of foreign animals, not only as a means of exercising observation, but in practical use.

In the same way expensive atlases (orbis pictus) would be profitably replaced by visits of children to workshops where artizans might exhibit their handicrafts to the little guests.*

CHAPTER II.

Speech and Writing.

Learning language is something far more important than learning languages; and all the praise that is bestowed on the dead languages as a means of culture, applies with double force to the mother tongue, which might be more fitly called the Language-mother. Every new language is understood only by comparison and contrast with the one first learnt, the primitive symbol being only re-symbolised;† thus the newer

---

* The principle laid down is of vital importance; namely, the value of first-hand experience in education. For visits to workshops we might even substitute actual hand-work, and the experiment has been successfully tried in some of our English Schools for Boys.

† Richter means that as words call up images of things, and hence are symbols of them, words of a foreign tongue first call up the equivalent in the mother-tongue, and then the thing; hence they are symbols of symbols.

language is not formed on the model of the *new*, but all model themselves upon the oldest, the native, tongue. Name to the child every object, every sensation, every action, if necessary even with foreign words (for to the child all are as yet equally foreign), and especially arouse the attention of the child who watches you, and give clearness to his perception by nicknaming all your acts where possible. A child has such a love of listening that he will often ask you about things that he knows quite well, in order to listen to you; or he will tell you a story in order that you may tell it to him again. By giving names, external things are conquered, like islands, and names were made for that purpose of old, as the beasts were tamed by giving of names. Without the defining word, the mental index-finger, the marginal note, the expanse of Nature would stand before man like a quicksilver column without a barometer scale, and no movement of the column would be noted. Language is the finest line-drawer of infinitude, the water-parting of chaos; savages show the importance of this dividing power, for with them a word often contains a whole sentence. The village child is inferior to the town child merely in the poverty of its words, which creates a solitude. To the dumb beast the world gives one impression, and it does not even count "one" for want of a word for "two."

Let everything material be mentally and physically divided and analysed before the child in the first decade of its life, but not anything spiritual, for this exists only once, namely, in the child himself, and dies easily without a resurrection under the dissecting knife, while material objects return to us newly born every day.

The mother-tongue is for children the most innocent philosophy and exercise in reflection. Talk much and very accurately, and enforce accuracy upon them in affairs of every-day life. Why do you wish to first begin culture by means of a foreign language ? Attempt occasionally longer periods than the short childish sentences of many educators, or the hackneyed ones of some French authors, an unintelligibility which is cleared up by their merely unaltered repetition exercises and strengthens the mind. Even little children may be sometimes exercised by the puzzles of contradictory words ; for instance, " I hear this with my eyes," " this is truly fine ugly." Fear no unintelligibility even of whole sentences, your mien, your accent, and the desire in them to understand, clears up one half, and this explains the other half by the aid of time. Accent is with children as with Chinese and cosmopolitans, the half of speech. Remember that they understand your language earlier than they can speak it, just as we do Greek or any foreign tongue. A child of five understands the words " yet," " indeed," but just try once. to give an explanation of them, not to the child, but to the father ! A single " indeed " would puzzle a little philosopher. If an eight-year-old is understood in his more highly developed language by a three-year-old, why will you narrow your speech to his babbling? Speak always some years in advance of him * (do not geniuses speak to us centuries in advance?) speak to the one-year-old babe as if he were two years, to the latter as if he were six, as the difference of growth is in inverse ratio to the years. The educator should remember that the child carries one-half of his world all complete in himself (namely, his moral and metaphysical objects of contemplation), and that just on this account language, armed with only material images, cannot give, can merely illuminate his spiritual ideas.

Pleasure as well as precision in talking with children should be derived from their pleasure and accuracy. We can learn language from them just as we can teach them by speaking; bold and yet correct word-formations are to be heard from their lips; for instance, I have heard from three-year-old children: " the beer-casker," " stringer," " flying-mouse " (certainly better than our " bat ") " the music-fiddles," " the light snuffs

---

* Teachers in schools need perhaps a warning not to push Richter's injunctions to the other extreme. Language " over the heads " of children falls like rain upon the rock. The error he would have us avoid is the mistaking of slipshod inaccurate speech for simple. The best rule is, in introducing an idea or subject to children, to use only words that they are perfectly familiar with, and gradually bring before them the condensed or so-called " technical " expression which they will then be glad to learn and remember.

out," "in the end I shall be quite too cleverer," "see, how one o'clock it is already."

For language-culture it is also necessary, at least later, that the faded old-world images should be brought back to be looked at with loving eyes. A young person says for a long time, " all made on the same last," " fishing in troubled waters," until at length he finds the reality—the last at the shoemaker's, or the fishing on a rainy day, and is greatly astonished that a stable reality underlies the transparent image. . . .

Fichte in his " Discourse to the German nation," lays too little stress upon the power of naming and the A B C of external observations or of objects, and he demands it merely for inner sensations, because, he thinks, the child names the former for the purpose of communication only, not for the better understanding of them. But it appears to me a man would lose himself in the starry firmament of outward perceptions, if he did not group these scattered lights into constellations and analyse the universe for his consciousness by means of language.

Our ancestors ranked a very foreign language (Latin) among the forces of education; and although their motives were pedantic, the result was advantageous as a means of mental gymnastics. The dictionary of foreign words truly does little for culture, except so far as light is thrown by them on our own; but grammar, the logic of speech, the first philosophy of reflection, does far more, for it exalts the signs of things into

G

things themselves, and forces the mind, being thrown back on itself, to observe its own method of observation, *i.e.* to reflect.

To unripe age this power of reflection is more easily obtained through the grammar of a foreign tongue than through that of our own, which is more closely blended with sensation,* therefore logically cultivated nations learnt first to construe their own language by means of a foreign tongue,—Cicero went earlier to the Greek school than to the Latin. When Huart asserts that a good head learns grammar with the greatest difficulty, he can only mean, unless he confuses dictionary with grammar, a head formed for business or art, rather than for thought. Every good grammarian is partly a philosopher, and only a philosopher can write the best grammar Thus the grammatical analysis of the old schools only differs in its subject-matter from Pestalozzi's " visible series." Consequently a foreign language, particularly the Latin, is among the healthiest exercises of the power of thinking.

---

* Cf. D'Arcy Thompson, in his " Day Dreams of a Schoolmaster ": " English is not the language upon which to found general and comprehensive ideas of grammar, such as may facilitate the after-acquisition of any modern language. You would never inculcate ideas of filial duty upon a child, by continually obtruding upon him impertinent mention of his own parents. You would tell him amusing and instructive stories of other children and *other* parents. Even so with grammar."

Writing. Since writing symbolises the symbols of things, it isolates and illuminates ideas more precisely than speaking. Spoken words teach more quickly, writing more uninterruptedly and accurately. This is true of all degrees of writing from the writing which the writing-master teaches to that which approaches the work of an author. Since it is certain that our imagination is more an inward seeing than an inward hearing, and our metaphors themselves play upon an instrument of colour rather than of tone, therefore writing which remains before the eyes must be of more lasting use for the production of ideas than fleeting tones. . . . Let the child write his own thoughts sooner than copy yours, in order that he may exchange the heavy, ringing coins of speech into convenient paper-money. But spare him copy-book texts as they are usually set—for instance, with praises of industry, of schoolmasters, of some old hero—subjects, in short, which the master could handle no better than his pupils. Every such representation is poisonous without a living subject and motive to deal with it. If even men of genius, such as Lessing, Rousseau, have required some living occurrence to suggest the text of their occasional poems (in the true sense of "occasional"), how can you ask of a child that he should dip his pencil in the sky-blue of indefiniteness, and therewith paint the vault of heaven in such a manner that the invisible ink should at last appear as Prussian-blue. I do not understand the schoolmasters. Shall human beings, even in childhood, preach only on appointed Sunday-texts and never choose any for themselves in the Bible of nature? A similar mistake is made by those who set schoolgirls to write letters in order to teach them the epistolary style; an unsealed letter is already half untrue. A nothing writes to a nothing! The letter written at the bidding of the master contains only the ghosts of thoughts, and it is well if the child does not become accustomed to insincerity by this talking to order. If letters must be written, they should be to real people upon a definite subject. But why this trifling, since one learns to write nothing more easily than letters, as soon as the necessity and material for them is present? Writing a page excites the desire of culture more than reading a book. Many readers of select school-libraries are not able to write a satisfactory notice of an accident, and a request for charitable assistance for a weekly paper. It is true that many good writers are poor speakers, they are like great merchants in Amsterdam who have only an office instead of a warehouse, but give them time, they will get you anything by writing for it. Corneille spoke lamely, but made his heroes speak all the better. I close this chapter, as a certain Indian began his book, by saying, "Blessed be he that invented writing."

CHAPTER III.

Attention and Generalisation.

Bonnet calls attention the mother of genius, but it is her daughter; for whence should it arise if not from the marriage (concluded in heaven) between the object and the corresponding aptitude. Therefore genuine attention is as little to be secured by preaching and flogging as an aptitude. Swift in a musical academy, Mozart in a philosophical lecture-room, Raphael in a debating club—could you get all these men, though men of genius and of mature age, with powers of reflection, to lend an attentive ear to such important things as arts, science, politics? And yet you expect and demand it for petty objects from children whose powers are inferior as well as immature! At most you may desire that the object of your attention which, like that of a man of genius, is a matter of caprice, should become that of the child's.

If you associate the object of the child's attention with reward or punishment, you have rather given place to another motive, that of self-interest, than given an incentive to the desire for improvement, at most you are working for the *memory.* No sensuous enjoyment or discomfort marks out the path into the kingdom of *mind.* "But what is to be done?" ask the teachers, instead of asking first, "what is to be avoided?"

The regulations of the Jesuits' Order forbid them to study longer than two hours at a time. But your school regulations command the little ones to study, that is, to be attentive, as long as you elders can teach ; it is far too much to demand, especially when one considers the young senses open to the universe, the cheerful murmur of life in the market-place, the moving boughs full of blossom at the schoolroom windows, the sharp streak of sunlight on the dull schoolroom floor, and the certainty on Saturday that there will be no afternoon school. A child may take the greatest interest in your instructions, but not just to-day, or not at this or that window, or because he has just seen or tasted something fresh, or because his father has promised or refused a trip into the country, or because the last instance of inattention brought down a punishment, and the child is thinking now more vividly of the punishment than how to avoid it.* . . .

Novelty is the source of attention in children, but novelty and repetition are antagonistic forces ; whilst repetition is, for obvious reasons, the mainspring of

---

* Richter omits to note that attention in grown persons is, or ought to be, much more under the control of the will than in children ; hence adult students do not need the stimulus of novelty to keep alive interest. It should be a recognised aim in education to develope the will in this direction.

schoolroom instruction. An important distinction is
to be made between the attention common to all, and
that special to men of genius. The latter must be
recognised and fostered, but cannot be created. Pay
attention, teachers! to children's attention, in order
that you may not demand from them that which is
utterly opposed to the genius which surprised you
with its force and lightning flashes, demand, that is,
from a Haydn a painter's eye, from an Aristotle a
poem. This instinct-like attention, waiting until it
meets its proper object, explains many apparent ano-
malies such as these, that the deep-thinking Thomas
Aquinas was called in his youth a bullock; the mathe-
matician Schmidt remained thirty-eight years a mere
artisan through incapacity for study and business.
Good trees bear at first only woody branches, not
fruit. Later on things proceed more swiftly, and
whilst learning and talent dig their gifts with effort
like gold out of the depths, genius presents his like
jewels gathered easily out of loose sand.

On the other hand, the kind of attention that we
may call universally human has less to be awakened
than to be divided and condensed; even careless children have it, though in them it is open to impression on
all sides. The child in the world, so full of novelty to
it, is like a German in Rome, or a pilgrim in Palestine.
It is not possible to give attention to everything; no
ball can be seen on every side at once. That passive
faculty of attention before which the trackless universe

stretches, is exalted by you into an active power by
directing it to a definite object which you at the same
time convert into a riddle, and therefore make attractive.

Let us continually ask *why*, of children ; the teacher's
questions find more open ears than their answers.
Secondly, you must, like Pestalozzi, make the object
clear through the magnifying glass of analysis ; and,
thirdly, reconstruct it, as he did ; thus the child will
bring his own activity into play, and attention will
follow of its own accord.

Then follows a discussion of the com-
parative merits and functions of Mathematics
and Philosophy. The author shows that
mathematical studies ought to precede philosophical, and has something to say about
the advantages of Pestalozzi's system, for
this very reason that the Swiss reformer
recognised the suitability of mathematical
ideas to form the staple of instruction in
early years.

That calm, cold calculation and mensuration, which
does not seek premature information concerning the
three giants and rulers of knowledge, God, the World,
and Self, which rewards each sowing moment with a
visible harvest, which neither excites nor represses

desires and wishes, and yet meets with examples and
materials for exercise in every spot of earth, and for
which no child is too young since the science grows
from what is small and simple, like the child himself.
Thus Pestalozzi's slow and luminous accumulations of
arithmetical and geometrical relations teaches the
child to carry a growing burden like the calf of Milo
(the athlete carried daily, it is said, a growing calf, so
that in time he was strong enough to bear the full-
grown beast). Pestalozzi in fact has inscribed over
life, as Plato over his lecture-room, " Only geometri-
cians may enter here."

Hence the reproaches against this reformer that he
has founded no school of the prophets nor of poets, are
merely eulogies upon him, and it were evil if he could
answer them. For it is just our misty, inconstant age,
fuller of dreams than of poetry, of fancifulness than
of fancy, that needs the sharp eyesight of mathematics
to give firm hold upon reality.

Meanwhile what will Mathematics have
effected for the child's mental culture? It
is shown that the power developed will be
that of generalisation, or of forming models
or types in the mind; and this power is distinguished from imagination on the one
hand, and from fancy on the other (in the

language of modern psychologists, from re-
productive and constructive imagination).
Arithmetic and Geometry as taught on
Pestalozzian principles cultivate this power,
and prepare it for the work of other sciences
and higher mathematics later on.

An exercise which will be found of use in developing
this power of generalisation is the condensation of a
series of philosophical or historical statements, until
the pupil has attained epigrammatic brevity. As an
example take the sentence:—

"Popular authors do not at first make choice of
thoughts, but write them down as they arise; just as
in the majority of states princes are not chosen, but
rule by succession of birth." This may be condensed
into the form, "popular authors do not allow their
ideas to rule according to the elective monarchy of
reason, but according to the succession of primogeni-
ture;" and, again, still further: "In the popular mind
the empire of ideas is hereditary, not elective."

CHAPTER IV.

Development of Wit.

Until the body is developed, every artificial development of the mind is injurious. Philosophical efforts
of the understanding, and poetical ones of the fancy,
destroy these very faculties in the young mind, and
others with them. But the development of wit, which
is scarcely ever thought of for children, is the least
hurtful, because its efforts are easy and momentary,
and most useful, because it compels the new machinery
of ideas to quicker motion, because by the pleasure of
discovery it gives increased command over those ideas,
and because in early years this quality, either in ourselves or others, particularly delights by its brilliancy.
Why are there so few inventors and so many learned
men whose heads contain nothing but immovable fur-
niture, in which the ideas peculiar to each science lie
separately as in monks' cells, so that when the man
writes about one science he remembers nothing that he
knows about the rest? Why? Solely because children are taught more ideas than command over ideas,
and in school they are expected to have their thoughts
as immovably fixed as their persons, . . . though of
course the information which you wish to combine
must first be in the head. After the severe rule and
lesson-time of mathematics, the sans-culottish freedom

and playtime of wit best follows ; and if the former works slowly and coldly, like the action of wind and wave in producing geologic changes, the latter, like volcanic action, is rapid and glowing.

Indeed, the transition from Geometry to the electric artifices of wit, is rather a step aside than a leap across, as is proved by the examples of Lichtenberg, Kestner, d'Alembert, and, above all, by the French.

That wit in the nursery and the schoolroom should take precedence of reflexion and fancy is easier to perceive than is the means by which it may do so. . . .

Richter here gives a short account of his little school at Schwachenbach, already referred in the Introduction (p. xiii.), and of the method adopted by him to develope this faculty of finding and expressing analogies between things and ideas seemingly diverse. He gives some examples from the " Bonmots-anthology," which illustrate his plan.

A boy, G., of twelve years, with mathematical and satiric talents, said the following : " Man is imitated by four things, by the echo, by his shadow, by apes, and by a mirror. The windpipe, the intolerant Spaniards, and the ants allow nothing foreign, but expel it. The air-bag of the whale, out of which he breathes under

water, is the water-stomach of the camel, out of which
he drinks in time of drought. Stupid people should
not be called asses, but moles, because it is only their
understanding that is not human. If calculations were
longer, we should have to make logarithms of logarithms."

His younger brother of ten and a half said : "God
is the only perpetuum mobile. Constantinople looks
fair from a distance, and is ugly near at hand, and is
built on seven hills ; so is the planet Venus brilliant
from afar, but spotted when looked at close, and full
of mountain peaks."

Their sister, W., of seven years, said : "Every night
a fit seizes us, in the morning we are well again.
The world is the body of God. When the pulse goes
quickly people are ill, when slowly they are well ; in
the same way, when the clouds go quickly they betoken
foul weather, when slowly, good weather."

My school was a Quaker's church, where any one
might speak ; the most stupid adorned themselves
most ; just as insects which are the most stupid crea-
tures are the most gaudy. Sometimes there were
several fathers and mothers of the same idea, one spark
kindled another, and they justly claimed to share the
honour of standing in the Bon-mots-anthology.

Slavishness troubles all the salt-springs of wit ;
therefore those teachers who, like weak princes, main-
tain their authority only by censoriousness and severity,
had better perhaps choose recreation hours in which

to make the little ones witty. The author of "Bon-
mots-anthology," permitted his school to exercise its
wit upon, though not against, himself.

Chapter V.

Cultivation of Reflection, Abstraction, Self-consciousness.

With respect to these powers the author
says :

I can be brief over the most important matters, for
the time and the libraries are prolix enough over them.

He then comments on the prevailing
fashion of self-scrutiny and introspection,
and shows it to be dangerous for immature
minds.

If they are of poetic or philosophic natures, such
introspection must be decidedly postponed until the
glowing time of passion, in order that the child may
lead and preserve a fresh earnest life. But children
of merely commonplace and active dispositions, for
whom the outworks of the material world are not so
easily demolished, these you may drive back five years
sooner into the inner citadel of their individuality by
means of Language, Logic, Physiology and kindred

studies, that they may learn to look upon their lives from above.

The inner-world is a medicine or antidote for the man of business, just as the outer world is for the philosopher. The poet's art is for both the higher remedy, as the blending of both worlds, since by it that more healthy reflection and abstraction is attained which raises man above necessity and time to a higher view of life.

CHAPTER VI.

On the Cultivation of Recollection, not of Memory.

The distinction between Recollection and Memory is more thought of by moral philosophers than by educators. Memory is merely a receptive, not a creative, power. Of all intellectual faculties it is the most subject to physical conditions, since all causes of exhaustion (mediate and immediate, as bleeding and drunkenness), obliterate it, and dreams interrupt it; it is only to be augmented by the physician, since it is involuntary, and possessed also by animals; a bitter tonic will strengthen it more than a dictionary learnt by heart. For if it gained strength by acquisition, then it would grow with the hoarded riches of years; but it will bear the heaviest burdens just in the empty unskilled age, and carries them under grey hairs as the winter green of childhood.

On the other hand Recollection, the creative power, belongs to the empire of the educator, for it is able to awaken and bring forth an idea from the storehouse of memory, as wit and fancy can do also. It is a *voluntary* power denied to the brutes, obeying the intellect, with the development of which it therefore grows. The Memory may be of iron, but the Recollection only of quicksilver.

(The division into "Memory for words," and "Memory for things," is therefore falsely expressed, for he who could retain a page of Hottentot words could more easily keep a volume of Kant in his head; for either he understands it, and then each idea more readily calls up a related one than a word quite unlike,—or else he does not understand it,—he then keeps a philosophical vocabulary and makes use of it in every disputation, as certain students of the "Critique" have proved. On the other hand, Memory for things does not presuppose Memory for names, but only because one might speak of Recollection, instead of Memory for things.)

Recollection works, like every intellectual power, only in accordance with association, which does not however picture sounds, so readily as things, *i.e.* thoughts.

Read to a boy a passage of history and compare the copious abstract which he will give you with the thin residuum after a page of Mexican words from Humboldt has been read to him. Plattner remarks in his Anthropology that things in juxtaposition are remembered with greater difficulty than things in succession.* It appears to me that an animal would have the reverse experience ; since memory is for juxtaposition and recollection for succession, because the latter and not the former excites active attention by causal or other connection.

(Richter seems to mean that co-existing properties or relations—for instance the colour, shape, size, smell, taste, and general appearance of an orange—are held in the *memory*, whilst they are *recollected* in succession. He omits to note that in this case the successive recollections may take place in any order; whilst in the case of a true sequence, as of a flash of lightning and a thunder-clap, the order of recollection is fixed by that in which the impressions were originally received. Memory works here

---

* This subject first received the attention it deserves at the hands of Jas. Mill, in the chapter on the Laws of Association in his "Analysis of the Mind." See Sully's "Outlines of Psychology," chap. vii. p. 234.

also, since the sequence must be retained, otherwise it could not be recalled.)

In order to exercise the connecting power of Recollection, let your child from his earliest years repeat stories consecutively, *e.g.*, some tale of his day, of a foreign land, or a fairy tale; hence at first the most diffusely told story is the best. Further, if he is learning a foreign language quickly, let him not learn detached words by heart, but a striking chapter that he has gone through a few times; his recollection will assist his memory, words will be remembered by their connection with other words, and the best dictionary is a favourite book.

A single thing is remembered with more difficulty than a connected series. Lessing's example, who always gave himself for a time exclusively to the same subject of study, confirms Locke's remark, that the best way to become learned, is to pursue only one thing at a time for a certain time. The reason lies in the systematic nature of the Recollection, since the subject of knowledge strikes its roots in such a case more deeply into the soil. Nothing weakens the recollection so much as rapid flights from one branch to another; it is often noticed that men become forgetful when they have to manage several different kinds of offices. Carry on the same subject with a child for a month uninterruptedly, what probable progress in twelve sciences in a year!* Disgust at sameness would soon be lost in the enjoyment of progress; and such knowledge, becoming ever more thorough, would offer the blossoms of variety from its own soil. At any rate, the beginnings of every subject should be so dealt with, those in which some progress has been already made being worked at occasionally for the sake of variety.†

Recollection by association of place, falsely called a "local memory," shows the necessity of connection; for savages are found to lose this local memory when transferred to unfamiliar circumstances.

For the memory there is also a mental talisman, namely, the charm of the subject. . . . Therefore no man has a memory for everything, because no one has an interest in everything. But the body sets limits even to this influence in strengthening the memory; remember this in dealing with children. For instance, if a bill of exchange for a million, written in Hebrew, were to be promised on condition of the very words of

---

* This should be read in connection with what Richter himself has said with respect to attention, and the influence of novelty upon it (pp. 86, 87).

† What is here said about working continuously at one subject, will be a valuable hint to teachers of young children (up to twelve years of age or so), if we understand him to mean that short lessons at short intervals are best. In this sense, the principle is acted upon by the best modern teachers.

the document being quoted in demanding payment, it would offer a strong inducement to most people to try to become the possessor, and yet the words and the form would fail him. . . . Similarity, the rudder of Recollection, is the rock on which memory is wrecked. Among related objects, only one can exert the charm of novelty. Thus the correct spelling of very similar words, is more difficult than that of words totally different.

This principle should be constantly borne in mind in early instruction.

The chapter ends with a word or two on the effect of emotional disturbance on the child's power of recollection.

Artemidorus, the grammarian, forgot everything when he was frightened. Fear, or even a sudden alarm, acts upon the mind as a pre-occupying force, so that the individual is rendered doubly powerless.

How then can teachers expect to gain a hearing, and force their pupils to remember, by threats and the cane ?

EIGHTH FRAGMENT.

CULTIVATION OF THE ÆSTHETIC SENSE.

CHAPTER I.

I USE the word *sense* instead of *taste;* taste, for the sublime and all allied to it, sounds as ill as smell for the sublime. Further, feeling for beauty is not talent for its expression; the development and strengthening of the latter belongs to the school of art for the art-gifted. If your boy, instead of feeling after and catching glimpses of beauties, is to produce them in the schoolroom, you will ruin him as surely as if he were to become a father before being a lover. Nothing is more dangerous for art, as well as for character, than to express immature feeling. Many a poetical genius has received a deadly chill by too early a draught of Hippocrene in the midst of his hot youth. Every clever man must, they say, make verses in his youth; as, for instance, Leibnitz, Kant, and others. This applies to those who make none at a ripe age; the philosopher, the engineer, the statesman, may begin where the poet leaves off, and *vice versâ.* But let the poet grow up to the stature of his model before he copies it. Let him, like the beautiful white butterfly, first live on the leaves of the schools, and unfold his wings when the flowers hold honey. When life has truly taken hold of the poet, even with prosaic circumstances, then let him take colours and paint therewith on the canvas, not colours, but his soul.

Men try to educate everything (themselves excepted) that will educate itself; and this just because the result is certain and irresistible, *e.g.* walking, seeing, tasting; but for the sense of artistic beauty, which really needs a school, one is seldom built. The child should be led earlier into the realm of beauties conditioned by the external senses — painting, music, architecture—than into that world—the poetic—whose charm appeals to the inner sense. Educate, above all, the German eye, which lags so far behind the German ear.*

The child should be surrounded with all that is beautiful in buildings, dress, ornaments; and the author complains that the State does not provide means of education for its citizens in this respect.

So far as poetry is concerned, he would not have the highest form pressed too early on the child's attention.

---

* Might not the reverse be said of the English eye and ear?

Up to the thirteenth or fourteenth year, the flowers of poetry are so many dried specimens for a herbarium. The child's mind is open to the individual elements of poetry, namely, rhythmic sound, picturesque words, happy thoughts, but not to the charm of the whole. Rhymes, full-sounding prose, are of most use in early years in awakening the sense of beauty in this direction. But when maturity approaches, and the joy-fires of life are kindled, and all the powers develope, then let the true poet approach; let him be the Orpheus to animate the lifeless, as well as to tame the wild beasts. But what poets shall the educator introduce? Our own! Neither Latin, nor Greek, nor French, but our own. Let the English choose English, the Germans German; and similarly let every people study their own literature. Only when we remember the poverty of the Dark Ages, whose expiring life was re-animated by the miraculous power of the Greek and Roman spells, can we understand the existing absurdity that, instead of forming and maturing the sense for foreign and ancient literary beauty by means of that which is native or nearly related and recent, exactly reverses the order.*

The most rapid comprehension and appreciation of

---

* Richter's reasoning is based on the important educational principle, "from the known to the unknown"; he is extending the application of it to the training of a complex emotion.

the fine gradations of colouring in a poetical work, the keenest sympathy with its subject, is only possible for one of the poet's own countrymen; and if the reality attaching to one's fatherland assists the poet to lay on the colours, it will also assist the reader to see them.

The author says, in his " Unsichtbare Loge ":—" Nature educates our taste for the finer beauties by means of the more striking ones. The youth prefers wit to sentiment, bombast to reasoning, Lucan to Virgil, the French to the ancients. He is not wrong, in that he feels certain lower beauties appeal to him more strongly than they do to us, but only so far as he is less sensitive to the blemishes inseparable from them and to higher charms than we are."

After the " minor gods of the house and hearth" have been duly enshrined, the earliest poets of one's native land should be read—for the modern are soon read with too much facility to make adequate impression— thus patriotism will be deepened and the mother-tongue read in models of the language.

CHAPTER II.

Classical Training.

The author refers here to a passage in a former work, " Die Unsichtbare Loge," for a summary of his arguments against the devotion of the greater part of the school life to classics. These arguments have been repeated in many forms in recent years. The necessity for familiarity with Latin in the Middle Ages in consequence of its use in the Church, the Law, and other departments of the State, no longer exists, so that the battle must be fought from the point of view of culture alone. With respect to classical literature he asks :

Whence come the men who have presented us with such books as Wieland's Explanation of Horace's Satires, Voss's translation of Plato's Dialogues? Only men of sense, of power, of culture, by means of higher and greater studies than mere language-studies, —only Sunday children, as Goethe, Herder, have seen the spirit of antiquity ; Monday children have perceived, instead, the wealth of language and the beauty of choice passages. Is it then not folly to consider it possible for a youth of fourteen or sixteen years, even with great abilities, to be able to understand the harmony of poetry and deep meaning in a Platonic dialogue, or the worldly persiflage of a satire of Horace?

What is said about classic literature does not apply to the classic languages nor to Ancient History. These have their place in education, especially the latter. The fortifications of the city of God have been founded by the Ancients for every age by the history of their own. The manhood of the present age would sink to an unfathomably low level if youth did not take its way to the world's market-place through the silent temple of the grand times and men of the ancient world. The names of Socrates and Cato are pyramids of the power of the will. Rome, Athens, Sparta, are the three coronation cities of the giant Geryon; after ages must lift their eyes to the youth of the human race as to the primeval mountains.

He who knows not the Ancients is the creature of a day, who sees the sun neither rise nor set. The man can draw the history of the Ancients from their own springs; the child must draw from the man; with the one exception of Plutarch, from whose hands youth may receive directly the inspiriting palm-wine of antiquity. . .

In reading the classical or other foreign authors, the pupil should take first those which present only difficulties of language, to be overcome by perseverance and study; and last those which are subtle or abstruse in the ideas expressed, such difficulties requiring maturity of intellect to grapple with them. Hence Livy may well be read before Cæsar, Klopstock before Goethe.

NINTH FRAGMENT;

OR, KEYSTONE.

THIS consists of sundry disconnected remarks on various points dealt with in previous chapters. The last chord struck is in the same key as the first.

Enough! I spoke above of a hostile future for our children; every father holds out this prospect, which he has inherited from his own. Who, indeed, has been so blessed, when finally closing his eyes, as to contemplate two fair worlds, his own now veiled, and one left behind for his children? Ever will humanity, as a whole, appear to us as a salt-ocean which the sweet streams and rain-showers of unique lives will not sweeten; but yet pure water is as little lacking on the earth as the salt-sea; nay, it even rises from the sea. Therefore the more exalted thou, O Father, considerest thyself to be above the present age (whether rightly or wrongly), and consequently above its daughter, to whom thou must consign thy children, the more it behoves thee to bring a thankoffering to the previous age, which has made thee so noble ; and how canst thou more fitly present it to thy ancestors than by the hands of thy children ? For truly, what are children ?

Our habituation to them, and their often to us burdensome needs alone conceal the charm of these spirit-forms, which men call in turn blossoms, dew-drops, stars, butterflies. But when you kiss and love them you give and feel all their names. A child appearing for the first time on the earth would seem a wonderful angel from a foreign world, who, unaccustomed to our language and atmosphere, would look at us speechlessly, but pure as the heaven, like a Raphael's holy child, and hence we can always adopt each new child into the child's place, but not each new friend into the friend's place. And daily from the dumb unknown world these innocent beings are sent into the desert earth ; and they alight now on slave coasts, on battle-fields, in prisons, now in flowery vales, on pure Alpen heights, now in the most iniquitous, now in the holiest, century, and having lost their only Father, they seek one to adopt them here below.

I once conceived a poem on the Last Day, and the two last children.

Its closing words may serve for the conclusion of this work.

" Descend then to the earth," said the Spirit to two little naked souls, " and be born as sister and brother !"

"It must be very pretty down there," said they both, and they flew hand in hand to the earth, which was already wrapped in the flames of the Last Day, and out of which the dead were rising. "Look," said the brother, "those are very tall children; the flowers in comparison are quite tiny; they will carry us about and tell us many tales. No doubt, sister, they are very large angels." "Only look," answered she, "how that great angel is fully clad, and each one the same, and every where the dawn shines on the earth." "Look," said he, "the sun has fallen to the ground, and burns all around. Over there a huge dewdrop makes fiery waves, and the tall angels bathe in it." "They stretch out their hands," said she; "they want to kiss them to us." "And see, too," said he, "how the thunder sings, and the stars fall among those great children." "But where are the great children who are to be our two parents?" "Do you not see," said he, "how those angels sleep under the earth and then rise up from it? Let us fly quickly." And the children approached nearer the flaming earth, and said, "Look kindly at us, ye two parents, play with us a long, long time, and tell us many stories, and kiss us!"

They were born just as the world, full of sins, was perishing, and remained alone; they stretched forth their little hands to the flames, and at last even they were driven out, like Adam and Eve; and the world ended with the Paradise of Children.

FINIS.

www.ingramcontent.com/pod-product-compliance
Lightning Source LLC
Chambersburg PA
CBHW020753020726
47495CB00008B/2415